W9-BMJ-965

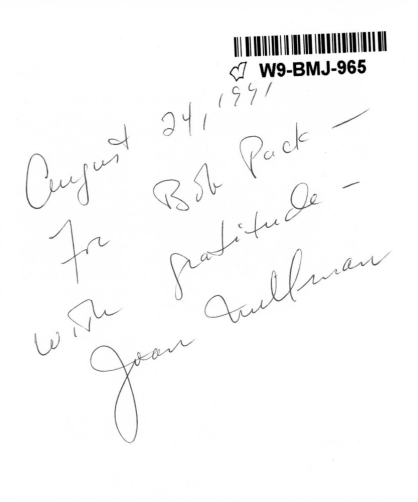

August 24, 1991

For Bob Pack —

with gratitude —

Joan Trullman

A BREAKTHROUGH BOOK, NO. 60

# THE EFFIGY

# THE EFFIGY

STORIES BY
JOAN MILLMAN

MIDDLEBURY COLLEGE LIBRARY,

UNIVERSITY OF MISSOURI PRESS
COLUMBIA AND LONDON

Copyright © 1990 by Joan Millman
University of Missouri Press, Columbia, Missouri 65201
Printed and bound in the United States of America
All rights reserved
All characters herein are purely fictional and all episodes are
acts of the author's imagination.

5  4  3  2  1    94  93  92  91  90


Library of Congress Cataloging-in-Publication Data
Millman, Joan.
    The effigy : stories / by Joan Millman.
      p.  cm. — (A Breakthrough book ; no. 60)
      Contents: The effigy — Custody — Esau's legacy —
Where touching is a talent — Equations — Diminishing
returns — To save and protect — Craving luster.
    ISBN 0–8262–0755–3 (alk. paper)
    I. Title.  II. Series.
PS3563.I422838E44  1990
813′.54—dc20                                          90–38758
                                                           CIP


Some of the stories in this collection originally appeared in
the following publications and are reprinted here with their
permission: *Carolina Quarterly, Cimarron Review, Ascent,*
and *Virginia Quarterly Review.*

∞™ This paper meets the requirements of the
American National Standard for Permanence of Paper
for Printed Library Materials, Z39.48, 1984.

Designer: Darin M. Powell
Typesetter: Connell-Zeko Type & Graphics
Printer: Thomson-Shore, Inc.
Binder: Thomson-Shore, Inc.
Type face: Galliard

*TO THE MEMORY OF MY PARENTS*

Anna Aronson Michelin, who encouraged me to try anything
I wanted to do and, most especially, not to give up
and
Julius Michelin, who passed on to me his zest and intellectual
curiosity and, most especially, his love of books.

# CONTENTS

# ACKNOWLEDGMENTS

To my mentors: Noah Gordon, Rose Moss, Rosellen Brown, John Gardner, John Hawkes, and R. V. Cassill.

To those who gave me free office space in which to write: The Learning Center for Deaf Children, The Marist Seminary, Jay Gordon, and the Public Library, all of Framingham, Massachusetts.

To those who provided funding: Brown University; the Yaddo Conference; and The Bread Loaf Writers Conference, Middlebury College.

To all the special "J's" in my life.

To Dr. Abraham Kaye for his early encouragement.

And most especially to Gordon Weaver, who selected these stories for The Breakthrough Prize.

# THE EFFIGY

# THE EFFIGY

———

Come. Wake up. There is a mind yet. Skin to feel pain. Legs that walk. A tongue that tells. Bodiless, Dora calculated the effort to rise, to dress, to leave the apartment at last.

Now was the beginning, last Sunday at five o'clock the end. In between lay seven days as hazy as the cigar smoke that lingered still.

From the dresser came the girdle stiff with stays, a longline bra, hose that rolled on first so that, corseted, she need not bend. She stared into the closet. The foxed tweed, nipping its tail, was, no, too dressy. Her best, it was for holy days, Indian's summer that made her sweat. The flowered silk was, after all, flowered. The plaid jumper hung limply. She chose the black shirtdress Fern had brought her on Monday, that she had dressed in on Tuesday, Wednesday, and Thursday, and wore still on Friday, resting it on Saturday, and sat in once more on *shiva*'s last day.

Centering the matched mohair parlor was a wooden crate, traditional seat of mourning. Dora carried it now to the trash. She puffed the cushions, emptied the ashes. Cigars—man's nature between his teeth! Dora bit a reddish and swollen lip, nibbled on all week. Tomorrow she would clean. When she had the strength.

Ready. Gloved. Her hat, purse. So now leave. Wait. Maybe an umbrella. She moved to the mat, to the door, the steps. Stopped. Looked in her purse. The card, still there. Suddenly, Dora returned to the incinerator. Who knows, you might need a box. She took up the crate, deciding to store it after all.

Now she remembered the mirrors, shrouded according to

1

custom. Undraping the first, she peered deeply in. Who would look back? Anyone she would still know?

"Downtown the first day," Clara would tell Sylvia. "Couldn't wait to spend his money," Sylvia would return.

She clutched the card, blue curly letters imprinted on her memory, the card Joseph had talked about over and over. "Here's Bluestone's office. He has all the papers, you shouldn't worry. Bluestone knows what to do. From Bluestone you'll get honest advice."

Joseph had left Dora to a Bluestone she had never met, as if some Bluestone could ever be a Joseph to Dora.

The pictures on the walls, on the aisles, and on every product were clues to guide Dora through her needs. Lentils for Joseph's soup. Gerber's for Joseph's breakfast. No. The lentils and cereal returned to the shelf.

A small milk, skimmed. Good for the weight, Joseph had said. Why should a thin man worry about a little healthy fat? Milk without cream seemed a deprivation. In the land of milk and honey, would there be skim milk? Dora stood in front of the soup. Did it have hours-of-bubbling richness? Dora tried to imagine the steaming flavors of a giant Campbell kitchen.

She recognized a TV detergent by the bird on its label. Why a bird for detergent? To think of flying? For every woman to fly from the sink? Her few dishes wouldn't want a bird.

Dora picked up the *Evening News,* as had been Joseph's custom. He would read it every night after supper to himself and to her. Then she would spread the pages on a newly washed floor. She pushed her basket to the quick checkout. Six items. How much does one person need?

"Joseph, you're listening?" Dora spoke to the refrigerator. "I did what you told me, Joseph. Bluestone was all right. You said trust him. A man with a pointed chin? A pointed nose, too? He said the money will be enough. The rings I signed to Fern. One day extra I didn't keep the jewelry you gave me. Your sisters, if they were alive, couldn't say I took a thing. I took their brother, that's all."

The TV filled the night with tales told to themselves, as Dora stared but did not watch. Midnight was nine o'clock. All of Dora was stiff. A good night's sleep, rest, was the best medicine. She set the alarm for seven, a habit of nearly forty years. No, tomorrow she would sleep till eight. Tonight she would skip her bath, leave only her teeth to soak. She put herself into her bed, across from its empty mate. She lay in it but did not settle. Sliding from the sheets, she rose to turn the TV full. Dora looked to Joseph's bed to place the ache of her limbs. Her eyes closed, then, to the boxed shadows, talking, talking into the endless still.

Clara came to ask her for mah-jongg. "Dora, darling, you should get out. There's more than TV. Look, Sylvia and I will be next week at the shore. Your Fern is wonderful, but how much can she come? Dora, please, here's where we'll be. Maybe you'll leave early, darling, and spend a day?"

There had been no spring and Dora could not feel the summer. She was touched by Clara's offer. "The Private Eye," Joseph had called her when Clara reported the neighbors' comings and goings. For Dora the apartment was large enough. Let the Claras worry about the world.

She glanced now at the paper pressed into her hand. "Clara, I need new glasses. You'll read it to me, so I'll remember, and who knows, maybe I'll come."

Fern crossed town to see her once a week, but last week Roselle had Asian flu, and Fern had taken care not to rush the child to health. Dora watched for their coming, glad for front windows. When she saw them approach, the girl as tall as her mother, she stepped out to wait at the head of the steps.

Fern held Roselle's hand as she puffed up the three flights. "Over the river and through the woods to grandma's house . . ." she hummed, tracing her finger along the wall.

"Ma, now listen, Ma, life goes on. Lately you sound like a recording, no inflection, no gossip about Clara and Sylvia. You act like an old lady. Fifty-eight! Ma, there's still life. You can't stay with the dead. It is over a month since you went to arrange with Bluestone." Roselle flicked channels, while Fern flicked through the mail, mostly shopping news, a few bills.

"Ma! Ma, what have you done? I knew this would happen. With Pa gone, no faking it any more! To lean on him, to depend on him to read everything! We pushed night school, but you were too stubborn—" Roselle giggled, turned the TV louder, too loud, cuddling her teddy, sucking her thumb. "He tried with my books, but you used every excuse . . ." Fern twisted the volume down, scolding her daughter, scolding her mother. "Now, look. Subscriptions! Magazines! My God, Ma, that's the best joke of all!"

Shame, the shame of childhood stung her. Dora felt again the guilt of hot classrooms, erupting with restless children, too big to be held and past caring, school merely another piece in their piecework day. What did Fern know! She had not been Dora Leveroff, drowsy always from the needle's long and weary nights.

Dora's eyes filled, eyes that had been too proud to coax meaning from the printed word.

"Joseph, I changed your sheets today. The ones with the blue flowers. They'll wash together, they'll stay the same. You know, Joe, Fern means well. Don't be mad. She's right. Her life is no picnic, Joe. We at least had a whole daughter. For her, sorrow is every day."

"Mrs. Kramer? Rick Boisvert from St. Martin's."
"Come in, come in! I hope you like tea, I made fresh a kettle." Dora fumbled for a doily in the bottom drawer. Muffins steamed on the counter. She took up a starched dishcloth, her hands shaking as she wiped the china cups. Why should she be nervous! A skinny boy, only. Crooked

teeth. Hair could be brushed. A sweater and jacket like anybody. Lights in his eyes. Nice, when he smiles.

Dora looked about her sparkling kitchen, proud that with time to spend, she spent it cleaning house.

"My lawyer, Bluestone, will pay, of course, will send a check every month."

"No, your daughter made the arrangements. She called the seminary. The lessons will be part of my apostolic work."

"Aposto . . . ?"

"Volunteering—hospitals, day-care centers, that sort of thing. I can come twice a week to teach you to read."

"Oh, I can read! But my eyes, they burn when I do. My Joseph would say, 'Dolly, darling, why should you read and strain your eyes?' He was a kind man, Father Boisvert. Jewish men are good to their wives."

The seminarian grinned. "Call me Rick, Mrs. Kramer. I'm a long way from Father."


"He had books, Joseph, baby books. What if Clara and Sylvia come by when he's here? Fern could mind her own business, God knows she has enough! My age and I didn't learn yet, and now I should read. Like a six year old!

"The world is changing, Joe. Imagine Fern sending here a boy from St. Martin's . . ."

St. Martin's! St. Martin's filled an entire block with shrubs and lawns, stuck in a regular gomorrah of butcher shops, fish markets, and delis. Inside St. Martin's, black-robed men dangled beads and wore dresses. Boys came and went in black jackets, riding black cars—Why black, black! They were only boys!—If life as it is known took place inside those granite walls, its secrets were never pried. The Kramers blocked St. Martin's out as though it didn't exist. Every Saturday, long ago, she and Joe rushed Fern past its gardens the child shouldn't think she was welcome by St. Martin's.

Saturdays, in that time, had been for choices, for the park, the zoo, a show. It was hard for Joe not to choose the shop, sewing, seaming, pasting, cutting, fingers flying over fur. But they would remember the sabbaths of their childhood, when one rested religiously, whether religious or not, and on Saturdays Joe would work until two, giving half a day to the spirit of the Law, if not to the letter.

Fern would skip past them, eager for the outing.

"She's tall for her age," Joe would observe. "Or is that coat already shrinking away? Do all children grow so fast?"

"Why shouldn't she be tall? She gets the best!"

The girl would dash ahead and Dora would call after her, "Fern, Fern, don't run!" while Joe gently overcalled, "Run, darling, run. That's what legs are for."

"How do you know what to buy?" Rick teased, as he helped Mrs. Kramer unload. He put the canned goods on the counter, while she put the perishables in the fridge.

"The short word is peas. Here, see, a picture on the can. The letters look the same on the pea soup." She picked up the two cans and matched the words. "The long word is tomato," she pointed to the five red-and-white cans, a special that day.

"Chicken must be an easy one," Rick said, remembering his mother's cans with the chicks. Did many adults cook by guessing?

"Chicken soup, Rick, you expect me to buy from the store? What can someone named Campbell know about chicken soup!"

Rick's lessons were teaching by guessing. How did you reach an American-born woman with an eighth-grade education, who hid her handicap so skillfully that sometimes Rick himself believed she could read? Primers offended her. Newspapers frightened her. She lost interest in words he contrived. She was bored with the alphabet. She wielded coyness when her attention wavered. Nowhere in Rick's experience could he remember such a woman. More than teaching skills, he needed a secret password—a *shazam*—to unlock her stubborn pride.

"See Dick run, see Dick jump, see Dick hop," the words rattled off the page.

"Okay, Mrs. Kramer, good. But sometimes you meet those words in different situations. Let's see how they look in a row."

Rick jotted down the words: run, Dick, play, jump, see, hop. His pupil blushed, caught in the act of memorization.

"Rick, why should I see how Dick runs? Or jumps? Where will I write and who will get from me a letter about a boy who hops or jumps?"

"A letter, Mrs. Kramer? You want to write a letter?"

The magic word! Rick wanted to sing with joy. His teachers used to say, "To be a writer, one must be a reader." Rick's pupil would not be a reader until she wrote. He would make communication so vital, so exciting, she would be forced to the page at last.

"Who would you like to write to, Mrs. Kramer? I will teach you the words to copy for homework. When you write well enough, what letters we shall send to the world!"

"Well, Eddie, downstairs, broke his arm. It didn't straighten, so they put a special pin in, a miracle what the doctors know! Children like letters, and they are not fussy."

"DEAR EDDIE," Rick printed, "HOW ARE YOU FEELING?"

The seminarian, as if given wings, hopped, jumped, and ran all the way to St. Martin's.

When Rick had been coming for more than two months, Mrs. Kramer asked the forbidden question.

"A priest you're studying to be?"

"Yes, of the Sons of Mary, a Marist. We teach, heal the sick, assist the poor. We are banded together in one strong body, as Jesus himself came to serve, not to be served."

The woman winced. "Why? Why such a waste of manhood?" she blurted at last.

"Wasted? I'm doing okay with you, aren't I?" Rick laughed. "I must be doing something right!"

"Rick, Rick, what is more blessed than marriage? Who should know, if not a widow? For you no woman will bring hot tea and lemon when you're sick, or listen when the books don't balance. Marriage, Rick, is a partnership. Maybe not fifty-fifty. Sometimes the husband is the boss, when it's no; sometimes the wife, when yes is stronger."

Now Rick winced. "During our novitiate we ask ourselves, what are we missing? Or gaining? How can we serve more than one, share a wife with God? The community of brotherhood, I guess, Mrs. Kramer, gives us that 'cup of tea.'"

"You are healthy, Rick? I mean, you are a well man?"

Rick sighed. He knew Mrs. Kramer's direction. "When we take our vows," he explained patiently, "we pledge poverty, chastity, obedience."

"Poverty! My Joseph and I could be priests, after all!"

"Wealth corrupts, Mrs. Kramer. You have been rich in many ways. Neither you nor I must have more than we have."

"Obedience, I understand. Poverty, yes, but who needs it! But, Rick, this chastity. Yes, I know what it means. But why, Rick? Why?"

Rick ducked his head, not to meet her question, nor to confront it within himself. He folded his hands, one thumb a tattoo upon the other.

"Well, Mrs. Kramer, that's how it goes. When you take the pledge, they make you buy the whole package."

"Chastity, Joseph, chastity, chastity," Dora muttered, a singsong, calling it over and over to Joseph's bed, making of the word a litany to put herself to sleep.

Buying the new beds had felt like picking out a casket. The brands, even, sounded like funeral parlors. Joseph sat on mattresses, pinched ticking, looked underneath Slumbersnoozes, Dreamrests, Bidewells.

"A new suite?" the salesman beamed, a regular matchmaker matching couples to their bedding.

"Yes," Joseph fingered his tired felt. "Ha, ha, ready for twin beds in our old age."

He had been opposed to the idea from the first. "Now, Dora, a little heart strain, 'slow down,' the doctor said, not stop!" But to Dora, "slowing down" meant fewer steps, lighter bundles, other sacrifices as well. "Slow down," the doctor had said. It was a prescription the business had already taken.

He was sixty-two, his prime! Prime skins were the pliable pelts, taken at the peak of maturity, neither too young to be fragile nor too old to be dry. Forty years he had keened his skill, forty years to become a master furrier. When ranch mink was the height of fashion, he'd precisely let out the lush male backs, dropping them so the fine dark stripe filled the middle. He'd slice the inferior pieces at the stripe itself, layering them so only an expert could tell. He'd tip, feather, lighten, or brighten. Coats became jackets, jackets stoles, stoles boas, giving four generations to a single garment.

Now that man-made furs kept women warm, Joseph's talents were conserved, although that was not what conservation was about. Joseph and his fellow craftsmen spoke of themselves as an endangered species. To Dora, he made light of it. "We survived the Depression, didn't we, Dolly! So, nu, we'll survive Ecology!"

When the old double bed was taken, the new twin beds filled its space. Dora made them up in flowered sheets and matching blankets. As Joseph brushed his teeth, taking longer to gargle his nightly hygiene, she could sense his gloom.

She put her head on its flower bed. How strange to be alone! Joe bent to kiss her. He turned his covers, stretched for a long time on his back.

"Dolly, you okay?"

"Mmmm, Joe. Let me sleep."

"Dolly, the mattress, it's good and firm? You're comfortable?"

"Sure, Joe. Go to sleep. You need to rest."

Joe rolled to his side, rolled back, turned to face her. A sigh blew between the beds. He reached an arm to Dora. Holding her hand across the gulf, Joseph fell away to dreams at last.

As the lessons went on, the teacher praised her progress.

Dora had not been so exhilarated since the Piper Cub at the fair. The breathless soaring had caught her heart in midbeat, and Joseph had teased her for being born too soon. Reading was like that. Like flying!

In Dora's kitchen they wrote and read letters. "Please note a mistake on my bill this month" to the telephone company. Or to the department store, "You have billed me three times for an ironing board. It never came." Items that puzzled them were referred to Bluestone, the attorney. "Dear Sir, Will you please give this matter your consideration?" When there was no business, they wrote to each other.

Dear Mrs. Kramer,

Your food is delicious. I am getting too fat for my clothes. Please consider my vows of poverty. I cannot afford to buy a new jacket.

Your friend,

Rick.

Dear Rick,

Can you come to my plas Toosday, ins, insted not Wensday. Fern is leeving Roselle here and the TV will be two loud.

Sinsearly,

Dora Kramer.

Rick was delighted with her long sentences, overlooking the spelling. That would come, he assured her. She was reading, reading! Something had clicked and she was running with it, driven by the magic of words.

Dear Rick,

I am woryd about this preest bizness. Who will give you children?

Sorry for asking.

Best wishes,

Dora Kramer.

A man's pleasure for his children even the worry doesn't take away. Dora looked long and sadly at Rick. Thin, dark, in the way women loved. They would call him Father, and he would never be one.

"To you, my young teacher, I'll make a confession. Confession. Isn't that how you get the little crackers? A golden girl called me mother and I never was. For me no stomach felt a baby growing. Rick, whose life is still in front, you are not a woman. You can give up a child who calls you Father with a real son's voice. Ah, that's how it is to be young! As how young was young when a handsome Joseph Kramer—handsome because he was smart, smart!—proposed to an ignorant Dolly Leveroff. A proposal not only to marry, but to become a mother on my wedding day . . ."

She had worked five years in the shop, so still only the Singer buzzed her presence. As muskrat and beaver, baum marten and seal, caracul and sable rose and fell about her, she'd fancy herself a White Russian, preening in fur.

His sisters treated Joseph like an apprentice. Not enough to master the craft of fur, they tutored him in the art of women. "Tell them they look beautiful, what else do they want to hear? Do they wear fur to keep warm?" Joseph, high-school-graduate, business-courses-at-night, a charmer in a quiet reserved way, would snare the women. The little skins would leave one trap for another.

When Joseph himself was snatched, the shop girl, Dora, was not invited. Yet he remembered for her a piece of wedding cake. "You'll put it under your pillow," he smiled, "and who knows?" And who knew that not a year later, Joseph Kramer would bury the woman whose entire marriage was spent resting for the delivery of their child?

Parenthood numbed his grief. Who would care for the infant? Ten years older than the plump seamstress, Joseph saw Dolly for the first time. How long had been his wait for childbirth; how he longed now for carnal solace. Hunger and shame seared him. What was his greater need: the flesh of his flesh, or his flesh?

". . . So I made a promise, Rick, and I kept it. I raised Fern and never had a baby of my own. That was what Joe wanted. His sisters thought I stole him from his memories, a wife not cold enough to be forgotten. We fed Fern mother's milk from Beth Israel. One mother gave the infant life, another nourished her, but I, I was the only mother she knew." Dora thought suddenly of the flawed Roselle, her sweetness, her trust. "Still, God help me, not even three mothers could keep from Fern the Evil Eye."

Dora's sorrow was older than a widow's.

"So, nu, not everyone gives birth," she granted. No one would marry Fern's Roselle. Some children were marked for purity.

Mrs. Kramer tasted the lead before applying it to paper. She strained to make the letters even, filling the blue-lined spaces as neatly as her own small world. Fifty years kept her from the expression Rick had seen on schoolgirls everywhere.

*Do* I know what a priest's life will be? And did you, Mrs. Kramer, realize what *your* life would become? For a woman, marriage is defined, a title, a job. *Should* I take the vows? Will that be the right decision, right for those I touch, right for me?

Rick watched her copybook struggle. He marveled at the joy of her discoveries, the simplicity of her wisdom. She was a grandmother, yet how eagerly she leaned on him. Could he share his deeper thoughts with her? Others, like his innocent pupil, had asked, no, accused, Why, why had he elected to be among the chosen? A caught look seemed to demand of the seminarian, "Are you better, stronger, than the rest?"

The long, dark halls of the seminary, at first austere, were becoming now his home. St. Martin's, a family of sudden men, stopped boys. The formal parlors, Sunday's public rooms, were rumpled with newspapers, filled ashtrays, and TV guides. Weekdays they squeezed from morning Mass the last dregs of sleep, boarded a minibus to college, and re-turned for vespers, meals, books, bed.

They wore civvies to class in a shared secret, were pleasant to their fellow students, but kept a witty distance. The seminarians clung to each other, accepted few invitations from classmates, and rarely invited one home.

At the cloister, they could let down, play pool or cards, shoot the bull. They talked about their past and present, but the future was hedged with wryness. They were but ten young men, the smallest class of novitiates in the Order's long history, a scrap of the Cloth's woof and warp, and upon them mortality hung like a dread.

Upstairs, each narrow cell housed a desk, sink, closet, cot. There, in the silence of late nights, soul-searching, not scheduled, nibbled the solitude. The training period was given less to learning than to stamina and dedication.

In the border town of Rick's Maine childhood, ruggedness was the style. Food was wrung from hard, dry earth, but not until he came to school had he felt another hunger. At the hands of the priests, he mastered classroom French, Greek to his Canuck, and when Rick discovered the cassock's other secrets—Cicero and Roland, Cervantes and Swift!—he knew a potato eye was blindness.

"A priest, is it, you want to be?" came the patois of his parents' pride. "An education money can't buy. Still, you are young. Time yet to change a mind . . ."

As Rick studied the woman, he was weary beyond fatigue. Time yet to change his mind . . . Would he? Would he defy the pull of averages, become yet another statistic in the Marists' failing charts? Would the heritage that sailed from France, and touched his boyhood with its only richness, shed itself on Richard St. Baptiste Boisvert and permit him to become a Holy Father, an honored and ordained priest?

As the kitchen lessons sped along, Rick spent less time correcting errors, more time talking. As he had challenged her with written words, she became now his foil with spoken ones. All the squelched curiosity bubbled out. Why, why, what mystery powered his faith!

"To be born into a religion, yes, what choices are there? But to take one step more, Rick, to make religion more than Sundays or holidays?"

Then he would defend. Such was the dialectic of his philosophy classes—he could read the teachings forever—but in a widow's spotless kitchen he could feel her cleansing probe.

Sometimes he would merely instruct. "Our ways are much like yours. We are not so different. Why, even our holidays coincide—Christmas and Chanukah, Easter and Passover. Our Lord's Last Supper is, in fact, the Passover Seder, and as it was then, so do we each spring, on Maundy Thursday, mark it at the seminary."

"And your childhood, Rick? You had this religion? It was not, like for Joseph and me, something to take up when you wanted?"

Rick wanted to laugh. Instead, he became a storyteller. He would show Mrs. Kramer what his life had been. Would she see it, as he did now, as another world?

". . . An empty seat was never a gap at school. It meant extra hands for the fields," he began. It meant termination—when the chair had filled before its keeper. It meant illness, laziness, drunkenness (yes, even a twelve year old could be hungover), pregnancy, and when welfare checks ran dry, abrupt departures. Truancy was an absent word.

Empty this morning next to Rick was the doodled desk of his best friend. Would Arthur have ever learned to read and write if Rick didn't spur him on with dirty notes? Father Dionne scolded the hell out of them when they were caught, and relented with, "At least you used good Anglo-Saxon!"

Every morning, after catechism, the teacher closed the door, punctuating the end of religious education and marking the beginning of secular school. He would rub his hands together, twinkle a private joke, and observe, "Adieu à Dieu, Bonjour à l'école!"

Now, though the priest had said the Our Father, had finished the Bible reading, and should begin the spelling lesson, his words seemed holy still.

"My young friends," he solemnly began. "Sadness has struck its ugly wrath upon us, and you must not grieve too much or too long for your lost classmate."

Rick heard fire, kerosene, stove. Rick dreamed Arthur,

burned, dead. He recalled Arthur's soused pa, his brother a run-off, his mother lacking, lacking even simple schooling.

"She stupid her, she stupid her," he ran blindly from the school, moaning doglike sobs inside the squatter, till Father Dionne came gently after him, cramped Rick into his arms, his grace the comfort of a sacrament. Into the vestments, that long day past, he pledged the first of his vows:

"School, Father, it teaches to be smart. Someday I'll leave this valley, go to bigger school, and know, and know!"

What would Joseph say to see them among The Forbidden? A Catholic seder! The priest, wearing white, stood behind a white-clothed table he called "the seder altar." He pinned a white lace shawl to her hair—how like the one her mother had used on Friday nights!—and Dora rose to bless the candles.

Rick, Roman-collared and in black, seemed by her side younger, too young. Next to him squirmed Roselle, a matzo blizzard falling beneath her chair, while Fern squirmed with pain. The wine was blessed, and Dora bent to the sweet sip, choking on tartness. "The altar wine, I bet," Fern leaned over to whisper. All at once, Roselle snatched her glass and lifted the brew. *"L'Chaim!"* she called. To life! Roselle, Roselle, sweet giver of appropriate surprises!

At the heavy-lidded singsongs of Dora's girlhood, her father had seemed to her a Moses, leading his flock toward their promises. His "ma-nish-tana—why is this night different from all other nights?"—had echoed all the sadness of time itself, but the words in the monsignor's mouth were a monotone, empty, hard, and strange.

The second sip went down with a sting. Why, altar wine was just a quick schnapps for priests! She spread an apple-nut mix on Roselle's matzo, and the child joyfully worked a sticky finger along its bumps.

They mean well, these priests, but what do they know? So flat, so flat. Dry like the wine. Passover was happy when she was young, and the singing was as real as the freedom.

Rick was called to the last of the reading.

"Had God brought us out of Egypt, and not divided the sea, *dayenu*!" It was the Jews' reassurance since Exodus of how little was their need: peace and freedom. "*Dayenu*, Lord." We are satisfied.

Rick's eyes sought his pupil. He wore the moment with ease. The passage fell swiftly, warmly, upon them. Here, among his friends, no longer a youth, not yet a man, he was showing off to Dora, pulling a magic trick, a child still.

So, Rick, French farmer from Maine, learning here your trade. A master priest you'll be. You might have been my son!

Dora reached for the undrained glass. Drinking, drinking to the rise and fall of young men chanting, to the flicker of candle tongues, she looked to the promise of their lives. It was for her too late for promises, past the time for plans. Dora sipped the last of the wine and yearned for the cry she had never heard, the voice that smothered in the fallow of her womb.

The hall bulb was out and Dora climbed to her floor in darkness. She blinked to adjust her eyes to the apartment, smiled wanly at the polished tables, the neat cushions embroidered so many years ago.

Dora sat heavily in Joe's chair. Her fullness, an enticement for a husband, was dead weight to a widow. She tasted still the bitterness of the *goyish* wine. At the Mass that followed the seder, the priest called the wine "blood," blood to wash down the "body." Dora poured out kosher cherry to wash away the blood.

"Joe, I'm drinking your blood. Joe, I washed your body, you washed mine. Joe, remember? After our first loving, you ran a bath. Soaking heals, you said."

Dora sat, shyly stilled. Would someone hear her spoken thoughts? She had talked aloud to Joe in the kitchen, in the next bed, called to him from the shower, and once held a long discussion with his absent presence while sitting on the toilet.

This evening, this long night in the Gentiles' world,

needed something more. She tried TV—only talk shows and old movies—and snapped the set off. The bitter taste repeated. She filled a tumbler with more of the crimson drink.

It was warm in her coat, her *yom tov* hat. As she hung the wraps in her closet, Dora plucked out the brown suit, the one she had not buried with Joe. Dora spread it onto the mohair. Too flat. Joe was thin, but the coffin had filled him out a little. His sisters would have liked he had at least then a little flesh.

The paper, filling the first leg, molded well. Two Sunday editions stuffed the jacket. The suit began to look like a little something, more like Joe. Dora lovingly shaped the head. It was hard to do. A head is not a ball. It has features, expression. Dora could not make the crumpled paper look like Joe. At last she tucked it into the collar, pushed up the lapels as for a cold day. A hat, now, to cover the not-so-Joe look. It would be Joe, just come in, too tired yet to take off his hat. Soon he'll pick up the paper, but first he'll ask, "So, nu, Dolly darling, tell me your day."

"I'll tell you, Joe. It is hard. No, I'm not complaining. Could you help it? It was your time, that's all. Still, Joe, it is easy for you now. No more worries. I got instead them all.

"No, I'm managing, Joe. No one tells me, helps me. Fern? What she carries she could be a hunchback! Even a simple decision till now I never made. Did I cook fish unless I asked, 'Joe, you feel like fish tonight?'"

Why was she standing? From the closet, she found it, the mourning box. Dora sat by Joe's feet and rocked. *Dayenu, dayenu.* Satisfied? A widow?

"I'm trying, Joe, but it isn't fair! Why did you go? To be alone, who needs it at my age, when it's for being old people marry! So, nu, you are safe, escaped. No more living, no more making jokes when you want to cry! So you left, left me alone without the words—poof—good-bye! The easy way. Leave a widow, and who cries bastard, deserter, *mumser*!"

Dora pulled the box closer, put her head in Joe's lap. She longed to feel him. His touch came to her. Dora thought back to the shop, how the fur tingled her flesh. Her breasts thrust their heat upon Joe, lifeless, lustless, forever gone. Sobs racked her. Dora let the storm in. She had not cried. She had not felt. She had not known desire of any kind. The total sweep of grief took her, rocking, rocking, on the little box, sole support for the bereaved.

"I hate you! I hate you, Joe! Is this my reward? I took you when you needed a woman, a mother, a wife! I gave, gave, everything! Joe, I raised another woman's child. In her you put your seed and were stopped in me forever!"

The effigy smiled. Was Joe recalling a Dolly young, a Dolly ripe, a Dolly eager? Dora pulled the zipper of her dress. She held her breasts to him. "Suck, suck the wine, my darling. I didn't mean it, what I said, Joe, dearest, dearest. Joe, lover, take! *L'Chaim*!"

Dora laughed. She was very tired. When had she felt so used? The figure seemed to be waiting. She found what he wanted in the end table. The cigar crackled, stuck in the paper ball. Its ash dropped to the flammable parts, slowly curling, cremating, the effigy of Joe. Dolly watched the brown suit singe, studying the brief flame of Joe's remains.

The sunlight of the starting season touched her pillow and Dora rose to let out last night's smoke, let in the bright new breeze. As after a long illness, the morning needed a cure for past neglects.

A thorough cleaning. No, maybe a paint job, new slipcovers. How tired the drapes, how worn the carpet! Dora glanced at the piled newspapers. Old news. Dora reached for the one on top.

WHITE HOUSE DENIES ALL.

Dora pushed on. Next were two lines of not-so-black print, easy to figure out. I'm reading, reading. Myself! I'm doing it myself! Dora laughed to the emptiness, the only witness to her solo flight!

She stepped lightly to the kitchen and took from the drawer the pen and paper.

"Dear Mr. and Mrs. Bluestone," Dora slowly, carefully, wrote. Was it spelled right? Yes, here was his card. "Please can you come and have dinner Friday?" It took so long, a passage of starts and stops. She stared at the words. Twice she changed her mind. She could phone the attorney. But to lawyers you sent letters. So, she would do the correct thing.

"Dear Mr. and Mrs. Bluestone," she read the words again. For the first time she wondered, did he have a wife? If not, would he come alone? She would ask Rick what he thought. She would show Rick the letter, and then she would mail it.

# CUSTODY

How carefully he removed it, bought for the anniversary party, folding its creases and passing its care to me, the custodian of my father's only new suit in ten years. Clean it, press it, he says. It's too good for his closet, certain to be vandalized by The Home's keepers. The suit comes back in its plastic wrapper and I hang it with my own, next to the others rubbing shoulders in the dark.

The suit—hell, it cost two hundred bucks!—was necessary. You couldn't let the old man out in what he'd wear. He'd protested. He might not need it again. Where does he go? But we insist, take it, take it. After the party he gives it back, while Darby, making him Chevalier or Chaplin, a sexy octogenarian, nibbles her grandfather's ear, strokes his neck. Myrna and I push the suit away, mistaking his meaning. Darby, wiser, interprets his intent.

Will we store the new suit till a next-time?

Yes, save it, he nods. With you it will be safe.

In a few days he calls, using the suit for his excuse. Did I pick it up? Did the cleaner do a good job? It used to be apples, pears. Then his watch, no longer faithful. Bring him a new alarm clock to replace the watch's fading face. No, bring him a clock-radio like the others have. What if the radio plays only rock—rocks in their head, he laughs—but it has also news, sports, weather. He hangs on the weather, though he does not go outside and pretends not to notice what days we pick to visit. Not when it is sunny. Golf is for the sun. Not when it is too hot, too cold, too rainy, too slippery. He is looking for a gray day when clouds press the conscience. Then one of us will come.

The next holiday we ask if he wants the suit. There'll be doings. Something to look good for. But he knows The Home's parties, the Shirley Temple drinks they trick him with. Dancing-school tots tripping in the recreation room. The women cry. Just like their Mary, Catherine, Eloise! He doesn't want to hear it. Keep it, keep the suit. Something more important may come up.

When Darby graduates, it is too hot for wool, too hot for bleachers. But he says he'll come. In the morning we bring the suit, already in mothballs. He likes the naphthalene smell, wakes you up! It takes him long to dress, disdaining help. Oh, why does he sometimes seem spry enough, as when he danced at the anniversary and when he mimics radio announcers and when he orders exactly what to bring, how much, how round, how juicy, the color, skin, texture, size, as if every morsel had the scrutiny of a royal taster! Dressing, he shows his age. Senility comes in flashes when we need him to stay with-it, be young, younger, just one more time.

The old man makes it, though, and, while Myrna and I sweat, looks dignified as hell. His tie, a little stained, is knotted tightly, the old Y-D tieclip holding it to its place. He could be back behind his counters, hovering over specs, Finest Eye Care & Eye Wear, nearly a doctor. Called that, at least.

The summer lays relentless parch on lawns and shriveled skins. Apple dolls on the front veranda, the women take their airing, drenched in Five-and-Dime cologne. The scents vie with sachet that sweetens drawers and powders dusted on their backs. Their skin is as clear as a bell jar, beneath which the veins are arranged in potpourri.

My father deals out postcards, enough to make a deck. Darby, nonwriter, noncaller, without benefit of any device of modern communication, relies on her essence to linger between visits, long spaces, the length of a whole summer, while she mountain-climbs in Aspen and whitewater runs some dizzying descent. Are we to be flattered that, still young, we do not require a missive from time to time? But somewhere there is yet consideration, drummed in with table manners and bedtime prayers. That shred outside the teenage sphere is offered one man only. Doc lays out Denver and Aspen and Las Vegas and Phoenix, pick a card, any card, if you want to know where your hoyden hides. Once above a Ouija board a spirit drifted as does my daughter through her chosen medium.

Myrna sips her gin and tonic through whitened lips. She can't imbibe unless businesslike. The visit given its due, we drive off to Myrna's wryness, "Where does he get it? That charm? Skipped a generation, I'd say."

A charmer, yes. Quick on the dance floor, slow to husbanding. Whatever genes are charted, given us on birth days, some of us draw the one marked "charm." Recessive, no doubt, cropping up in random generations. Manifested in Darby at sandbox level where little boys gave their hearts and sifters to her.

The suit hangs and there are no doings fine enough to spring it. Thanksgiving, he doesn't visit. His seat is taken by Darby's friend. Date, beau, boyfriend, steady, roommate—such words are now passé. He is her "with." Darby's "with" eats little, and Myrna begs him spare us leftovers.

Myrna is a sheath that never bends to one bite more. Leftovers are her enemy. She scarcely dents the bed, leaves little ripples where I make large waves. Everything about her is fine, fine-textured, fine-skinned. Her body has no hair, her hair no body. She aches to pierce her ears, but she has no earlobes either. No flab hangs from upper arms, no handles from her hips.

Ah, but Darby began life fat. Myrna fed her LoCal from six months on, yet Darby was never thin enough. She was forced to gymnastics, given extra swimming, and when the girl took Home Ec, Myrna stormed the junior high. "Eating what one cooks" shattered every weight-watching concept. The curriculum was altered.

* * *

Winter passes on the other end of boots, slush, fuel bills. Myrna has a continuous hack and blames my nicotine. I release my classes to independent study, letting the librarian spar with adolescent energy. Our social studies team rotates topics, sharing the intern breathing down our notebooks. The teachers' room is one long grumble.

My father wears a robe above his trousers, soiled, wrinkled, of vintage era. He takes his meals in his room, won't be cajoled to bland and formal dining. In the large hall, salt-free and Muzaked, the women bitch, cat, whine, pretend to comprehend what they can little hear. Spiced throughout, the fourth at table is a solitary male. The odds do not quicken the old man's appetite.

A rustle signals the arrival of his tray. To the volunteer he points out Darby's picture—a beauty queen! All the staff humor him. The nurses nicely call him Doc, but the doctors never do. The winter is long, long for us, longer for him. He has no interests. He used to go to OT to shape clay or stretch his arms to someone's yarn. Sometimes he'd riffle ancient magazines. He used to walk to the TV room where no one can agree and the attendant makes the choice. No, he does not need his suit. He stops mentioning it, though once he mutters, "Two hundred bucks shot to hell!"

Spring is here, waking all the trees. We are a family of arborphiles. When I was little my father talked about the trees in walks together in the woods, the woods that took him from his gentle calling and brought vigor to his stride. He'd point out each personality and let me in on lore he'd learned and stored.

How the ginkgo in the Orient was better off as male. The female's fruit so bitter, a gardener could be grateful for its sparseness. Was it once in thirty years or so it came round to its fecundity, dropping its smelly offspring, driving one away from its blossoms? To return to a barren stillness for some thirty years or more?

I'd wonder if they kept those female ginkgos in seclusion, like nuns in a nursery somewhere, and I'd wonder how they were fertilized and who if anyone gathered up their rancid fruit.

But then my father was off on another Oriental tale. Cows devouring redwood bark at dawn. Or was it bark off the dawn redwood?

As maples dripped toward buckets, we were silhouettes at dusk. I'd trot behind, filling his footprints, sharing tales and the last of daylight. Children of the woods, we hated to come indoors to the woman who was attached to things, her sewing machine, pickling jars, crochet yarns, crewel. Pine needles drop from shoulders; woods make mud on polished floors.

I in turn gave my daughter what my father gave to me. Darby collected leaves in a shoe box, the lobed, toothed, whorled, stalked. She'd dust her dollhouse with pine tufts and make of ferns fans for royal balls. Later the greens were bookmarks, and, even now, on remembered holidays, she presses inside a Hallmark greeting a leaf she particularly likes. My father tucks them around his mirror until they snap and crackle and are whisked away by cleaning help.

Now when I listen to the silver maple brush our bedroom window or watch the poplar's bend, I feel the heaviness and lightness of the trees and take comfort from their solidness or grace.

Word from the wayfarer at last. Nice of her to let us in on her latest acquisition. Most messages are ones of needs. This one proclaims a gain! After rationalizing living together, how good to know each other better, how mature and profound and independent and wise to opt for no-strings, she calls, gleeful as a hunter. "He said yes, he said yes!" Modern woman, she proposed to him!

Now another set of parents long-distance on the phone. We all try out for in-lawhood. Myrna is crying, "It is harder to be a mother-in-law than a mother," and the other woman's voice seems to sniffle in agreement. We fathers shake hands gruffly through the wire, wishing for cushioned leather to secure us, an icy glass to anchor pain. Mine is an Academy Award performance, loving that boy of theirs as if he were a boy of ours, but damn, I can't recall him from a collage of faces. The Easter weekender? Christmas sojourner? The college roommate Darby embroidered matching pillows for?

The picture on the fridge keeps me from TV snacks, reminding me that Darby's getting married. Myrna has posted the well-dressed mother-of-the-bride to hold her to starvation. She has bought the dress a size too small. Now she will cut, cut her rations as we once hoarded ours in foxholes, until she fits.

I let out the news at my father's bedside, but Darby has already sparked him with her joy. Of course he assumes I share this mood. We kid about the suit. See, Dad, good times! Plenty of good times!

It is not the wedding I mind, nor playing donor to the groom. (How can a "with" metamorphose into a groom!) What I mind is losing her. I, her first admirer, prep school for the real thing, how will I let go? Flick off fathering in a mere ceremony?

Caring is not as hard as pretending not to.

How easily kids let go of us.

My father sits by his cheerless window, staring like a monk in meditation. Here there are those who get religion. Last year Bruno wore his rosary thin, born-again to read the Bible. He scolded my father for his *Playboy*s, predicting hotter times in hell. The priest's last rites were hasty, vying with the Stanley Cup. Bruno's bed is empty still, awaiting his replacement.

I tiptoe in and watch the old man in his trance. Why, why does he not look up and latch me to his needs? The hard Swedish crackers, the crusty rye. A sweet that is forbidden or some bourbon for a secret nip? Never have they fed him well. He'd darkly hint of rampant felony. They steal from Medicaid. Chisel on Social Security. Cheat Welfare.

Darby insists he stand for portraits, so I try to lift him from his stare. This is for Darby, hey, hey Dad, you can do it. C'mon, Doc, give you something to look forward to. I have his suit and the nurse babies him into it. I do not recall either parent talking baby talk to me, and we never laid it on our daughter. It waits, then, for the other end of the line.

He makes the journey from door to parking lot, resting lightly on my arm. It seems a hundred miles—how wise were we to press him? In the car at last he smiles and is still. To fill the silence, I talk and talk and talk. I tell him everything, all the inane trivia that hits our academic fan. He seems to chuckle in the right places, and it feels natural for him to be my audience. In the car I am not my father's father; I am again his little boy.

Myrna calls me often while I am teaching. A bridesmaid has become pregnant, how could she! Another has run off with her professor. Can I spring for video as well as portraits? I am so tied up with meetings she seldom sees me—do I mind the interruption?

The ceremony will be simple, nonsectarian; the reception informal, light. Nothing stuffy for the contemporary couple. Why, then, are we in hock for an heirloom gown, an album of mock leather, and a covey of attendants to run up the florist's bill?

Myrna is running, running, forgetting to let her fingers do the walking. We fight in bed about the wedding. *We* ran off to escape the trappings and now my wife is a bride for the first time.

While Myrna stalks the stores, Darby blazes the trails. All winter she snowshoes the Audubon Reservation to seek her chapel. One afternoon, Darby, o lovely tree freak, comes in apple-cheeked with cold. She has found it at last, waves its Polaroid replica. Gnarled, old, blue beech. Its branches give out green protection. Beneath their spread the land's rise, like an altar, will lift the couple to their vows and there all of us will gather to watch our Darby wed.

* * *

The clothes strut across doorjambs, hanging above sills to keep from dusting up the floor. My father's suit on one, mine on another, the wedding gown on a third. Myrna's swishes as I brush against it, and in our bed I imagine their shadows dancers in a mossy ballroom gliding in a still spot beneath a canopy of boughs. A little girl now a woman and a little boy now a man, arrows shot from bows at birth.

Tonight is our last night. We are gaining a son. No, he is gaining our daughter. Did Myra thin her for this slaughter?
    Will she call me Daddy still or will she move steadily away?
    All the years of giving her some string, a ball unwinding away from home. Yet it could always be pulled back, like the childhood game of a purse left out with a hidden string to fool the finder. Snatch it back! Darby, treasure put out by Myrna to snare a man. How can I snatch her back and keep her? Fathers cannot cry at weddings. Only mothers do. Myrna sighs in sleeping sibilance, no trouble in her heart. Oh well, she's had her daytimes to dream and cry. I bury tears in my pillow.
    I listen for the bride to toss her fears in sleep but the only sound is branches, the twin sentinels outside our house. Will Darby remember to plant two trees by her own front door, as our forefathers did in early times, to symbolize the unity of marriage? Tomorrow when the question comes up, "Who gives this bride in wedlock?" firmly I'll call out, "We!"

He will not come. Not *will* not. Cannot. He is weeping in his bed and words at last are slipping out.
    This is Darby's day and her grandfather is as much her love as the boy who gets her pledge. Doc, stop crying! Your suit is newly pressed. There is a carnation for the lapel. A dapper touch to give you spring.
    Come on, old-timer. You can make it. I'll walk with you. She picked a tree near the road, a spreading dark and shady beech, not the deeper woods. Stop crying, Dad, please. I can't stand to see you cry!

He is crying and pointing. He is pointing by his bed to the floor. His slippers? He will get out of bed? Crouching on the floor is a bottle. A tube joins him to it. His words slip and slide, stop and start, oiled by tears. They make no human sound. Baby, baby, I hold him, rock him. This is my father and he is weeping on Darby's wedding day.

# ESAU'S LEGACY

It was Mendellsohn, he guessed, who started it with his note, the artsy studio kind. "That bastard," his father always called him, "that bastard-Mendellsohn-the-rabbi," all in one breath. His mother tucked the note in with the valentines and birthday cards she kept in a Whitman's box. "Have Robbie's BM marked," it said. The abbreviation jarred her. "See you at the meeting Tues.?"

Robbie liked to hang around when his parents talked. It excited him to be the center of it. Usually it was money or what his Aunt Elaine said or business. Now as the countdown for him was beginning, Robbie pretended he couldn't get a good picture, flicked channels, studied the TV guide, for an excuse to listen in.

The bar mitzvah was their island, returned to over and over. "Good Christ almighty, Elsa. I'm not spending that kind of dough. I'm not bustin' my ass . . ."

"But Arnie . . ." Robbie listened to the cadence of their voices, his father's straddling his mother's, leaving her frazzled in *buts.*

"A man! At thirteen! Forget it. Temple's okay for a little background, social contact."

"But Arnie . . ."

"Look, Elsa, forget it! I'm not pissing it away a second time. Five thou for my smart-ass son Nathan Breitman, and where is he? Playing the goddamn guitar, Christ only knows where!"

"But . . ."

*   *   *

29

Lying in his room past sunset, waiting for kitchen smells, Robbie copied Hebrew letters, cocked for ball scores following the news. Already the girls in class were giggling about guest lists, Jonathan Rosen bragging his bar mitzvah was to be by the Wailing Wall. Mr. Feldberg screamed not a one of them would make it, not over his dead body. Robbie rubbed the strange square signs with a wet finger, certain Feldberg never checked the work.

Dad was sure to beat his mother in the bar mitzvah fight. Then Robbie could drop out. If only his father would look in sometime, as when they were small, shadowboxing both of them in their bunks, a little soft-shoe and a one-two nuzzle to their jaws. If he stopped in tonight feeling like a little action, Robbie would say, "It's okay, who needs it? Let Mendellsohn-the-bastard keep his old bar mitzvah!" Tossing his Aleph-Bet to his p.j.'s huddled at the foot of his bunk, Robbie reached for the soccer ball, bounced it to the ceiling, printing the paint with waffles. Who needed it, glad rags, parties, girls!

Each spring Mendellsohn held an orientation. On Tuesday his mother begged his father to go. "Who knows, there could be changes in bar mitzvahs." At the meeting Robbie stared at Rabbi Mendellsohn. Something about him at least had changed. At temple model seders, Mendellsohn the rabbi always stood at the head of the line of girls and boys filing into the social hall, parting them like the Red Sea by sexes. Closing his eyes, he dipped and swallowed the seder plate morsels, in his black suit seeming to talk only to himself or God. Tonight he strutted in stuffed polyester, making Robbie feel mistaken about the words with God.

"Turtlenecks, well, yes," Mendellsohn fielded a query. "But we prefer ties for the father and son."

"For this I'm missing the Bruins!"

"Pork strips can't be prepared in the temple kitchen," Mrs. Rubin was told. "Mock pork, if you want."

"Christ, what a waste of time!"

"Party-Land does beautiful work," Jonathan Rosen's mother offered. "For a little extra, they give French service."

A fat woman nodded. "And with black lights, the baked alaska glows purple."

How mom had loved his brother Natie's! Aunt Elaine must have called every caterer in the Yellow Pages. He couldn't figure the big deal for the skullcaps to match the flowers or the fuss about everybody's clothes.

Suddenly the rabbi bent to his secretary's whisper and hurried away. A short man took his place, beaming a secret, almost. Robbie sat up. Maybe now they would tell what the kids do.

"While the rabbi has been called out . . . ," the speaker sounded oily. "About the donation to our beloved rabbi . . ." He coughed twice, smiling, smiling. "This year, with the cost of living going up, may we suggest two hundred dollars?"

That was when his father dragged them away. At the last "orientation," when Mendellsohn had been "called out," the pitch had been for one hundred. Cost of living! Where the hell did Mendellsohn-the-bastard get off?

When Robbie came home from camp, he expected to be told the plans. Even by September, nothing had been settled. The social management team, his Aunt Elaine and his Grandma Goldschmitt, was desperate.

"If money is what's bugging him, we'll find another temple," Aunt Elaine brushed off his mother's *buts*. Aunt Elaine could get a degree in bargain-hunting, his father always said, but could she shop for a cheaper rabbi, a sale-priced ceremony?

Again the Yellow Pages came out. Who would believe, Grandma Goldschmitt marveled, that Springfield, with so few Jews, would have six synagogues? "No wonder," she laughed, "they tell about the Jew on the desert island who built two temples, one to join and one not to!"

His aunt took charge. They would draw up a list. Tomorrow they would start their shopping trip.

When his relatives returned, Robbie, spread-eagled over the sports page, eavesdropped on their fruitless day.

B'Nai Shalom had a two-year membership requirement before bar mitzvah lessons could begin. Beth Zion's waiting list was ridiculous: you could be old before you could become a bar mitzvah boy. Israel in the Pines was so Reform it made Mendellsohn look kosher. Plus dues, they wanted $1,500 for the expansion fund!

"Well, we've had an education," his aunt summed it up as they left. "It's blackmail. No wonder *goyim* think Jews are rich, the temples themselves believe it!"

After dinner his mother brought the gin cards out. He hadn't practiced his clarinet yet and Robbie hoped she wouldn't remember. "Robbie, there is one little *shul*. But I don't know . . . the neighborhood . . . I don't like you going there."

"Aw, Mom. When are you going to let me grow up!"

The building, a block from the end of the bus line, looked condemned, at the least, cursed. Bent Coke cans lay about and newspapers fluttered against the crumbling cornerstone.

It must have been built in stages: brick here, granite there, clapboard on a still later renovation. The bottom steps were chipped away. It took a long stretch to go up, a hop to descend. Of the double doors, only one opened. On each was a matching stained-glass Magen David. A board covered two points on the left-hand star where the glass was broken, as if the missing points, the missing steps, were clues to the gaps inside.

Behind a streaked glass in a tiny office, no bigger than the Breitman powder room, an elderly man dozed over his prayer book. Soft snores rattled his bulbous nose from which hairs stuck out in tufts. From his mouth brown spittle ran, the residue from a stub abandoned in an overflow of past cigars lying in a jar cover upon the cluttered desk. Enormously fat in the middle, he was strangely thin in the extremities, like the clay figures molded by tots.

"A bar mitzvah!" the old man echoed. "Join the temple? Building fund? Nu, isn't it enough to bring a boy to God?" Lazar Fein beamed at Robbie two gold teeth from a face of wrinkles that was, like the building, declining in stages.

Looking inward to when time was young, he recalled the days of Beth Elohim's bloom. How he had arrived himself for bar mitzvah, a boy, yes, but already a worker on the streets five years before becoming a Jewish man.

Since then three generations of bar mitzvah youth had washed in and washed away. Now the black sea of the temple's neighborhood had engulfed the last of the Jewish families. Rodríguez and Martínez replaced Levy and Cohen on mailboxes. The Jews fled.

Ah, of all the *shul's* many lacks, saddest was the loss of its children. The young families had moved on. No bar mitzvah had been celebrated in years. At times, even, where were the ten men? Who could deny that Lazar Fein, *shamus,* sexton, janitor, teacher, substitute rabbi, could himself round out the required *minyan?*

He, Lazar Fein, would happily instruct the child. Yes, he could have him ready by his birthday. Robbie could expect to start next week. Tears pinpointed the teacher's eyes. The strangeness of the shul covered Robbie with sudden chill.

It was sundown. Now remnants drifted in for evening prayers, ghosts kept by covenants. The *shamus* announced the news, and the elders, igniting dying embers, began to bob the blessings, rejoicing, rejoicing in Robbie's coming. Taking up his own *siddur,* only then did Lazar Fein let go of Robbie's hand.

Riding the long bus route now, Robbie watched the rows of slab houses, the colonial split-levels, the raised ranches, corral fences marking their ranchiness. Plastic shopping malls, like neighborhood control centers, flew past his window, and the quickening of eateries—McDonald's, Pizza Hut, Wendy's—lifted him from the bland zoning of the suburbs. At last the bright new ring of commerce outside Springfield fell away to the dark town, quietly settling its soot in relentless layers of age.

"Nu, here is our bar mitzvah boy. A man, so you're going to be! Here you'll learn what it means—a man!" In Lazar Fein's custody, he began his preparation. The sunlight filtering through tenements on either side stopped at Beth Elohim's door. Robbie felt the cold and welcomed the wrap of the prayer shawl. Before the rabbi began, Robbie meditated in the small sanctuary. Mimicking the old man, Robbie bowed his head, let sports and school, homework and family, drain away to dimness. "Now." The stout man, no taller than Robbie himself, raised his gaze to his pupil. "We shall begin.

"Answer me, Robbie, if the Sabbath promise be kept, why does she descend at different times in different lands? Is there not one golden moment that is the Bride's time alone?" Who had addressed Robbie thus in riddles?

"If God wanted Man to rule His world, why did He give him Woman to rule Man?"

The bearded men of the congregation wandered in to audit Robbie's lesson, dozing in front pews, nodding their tarnished memories of the time when youth had a place before their ark. But when Robbie stumbled on a phrase, it might be Krokowitz or Stein or Morris who acted the backstage prompter. Were they once thirteen, he wondered, stepping forever away from a child's world? Robbie looked at Krokowitz, fingering his fringe with stained, arthritic knobs. Stein, so hunched his life was bowed in reverence. Morris, toothless, voiceless, all the holy words taken by surgery. With these elders, tightly wrapped, skulls capped, wound and bound, bent and leaning toward the holy of holies, Robbie swayed, feeling close to the wonders that were surely here.

He learned a ritual rock and roll, a monologue beseeching heaven. Fein took the Torah like a baby, unswathed its parchment. Then the elder and the protégé rendered the language of the sheepskin, the cracked alto a sobbing counterpart to the boy's girlish tones.

The intricacies of the little black boxes, bound by straps to his skull and arm, were revealed. For it had been written, "Thou shalt bind them upon thy doorposts and as frontlets before thine eyes." And revealed also were the mysteries of his desert people, as old as Moses as a boy, passed now to him, Robert Edward Breitman, from Lazar Fein.

"That's crazy," his father bellowed. "Hell, Fein's carrying things too far. Nobody takes bar mitzvah lessons that serious."

"But Arnie, Beth Elohim requires attendance Sabbath mornings. You know they won't let him ride. Mr. Fein says he can sleep at his house on Fridays and come home after sundown Saturday." But his father, fly open for TV's ease, mashed his cigar, reached for the Schlitz, and was already on the Yankee diamond.

Anyway, Friday was the Breitman card night. The men met for poker, the women played mah-jongg. He seldom heard his father make it in, but Robbie remembered a distant time when his return roused him like a nightmare.

". . . cheating, whaddya mean cheating . . . ya rotten hypocrite . . ." Natie's accusation bounced off the living room to Robbie's bunk.

"Clayman told me the whole thing, you lousy lying sonofabitch!" his father roared. Robbie crouched in his bunk, terrified to go down. In his sleep perhaps he had dreamed the fight, Natie sobbing—how Natie would deny, deny—his father yelling, his mother interjecting, "but Arnie, but Natie," playing the goat as always. Robbie heard a slap and his brother whine in Robbie's own perfected style. "Scared shitless . . . scared to give Ma a stinkin' penny, what does she ever ask ya for . . . we gotta play we're broke . . ." Natie's voice stabbed the night.

"Ya rotten brat, ya get everything ya want, don't ya? Who'm I breakin' my hump for, how do I know I won't get screwed into the ground? What do ya know about the world, anyway, big shot?"

The phone's sharp intrusion cut their voices off. "Yeah, yeah, sorry to disturb you, the TV louder than we thought." His father cursed as he hung up, and Robbie drifted off to sleep.

In the morning, Natie's leaving was felt at once, the wildness of dropped underwear and socks, boxes tossed about his floor, the rage unleashed on despised schoolbooks, the missing guitar a firm clue to the distance he had fled.

Onions. Chicken fat. Robbie didn't like the smell. Lazar Fein lived alone, a widower, in the basement of the building next to Beth Elohim. Since the congregation never rode on the Sabbath, proximity to the synagogue was essential. Fein's devotion was merely a step away.

"Nu, Robbela, you have memorized your Torah portion?" The dishes from the simple meal were left in the sink. The candles flicked their shadows along the wrinkled wall where a tattered tapestry was hung. The cement floor was cold. The place was cold, dark, and smelled. Robbie wished suddenly for the comfort of his room, his own TV—he was missing the championship match tonight—maybe he should have listened to his father!

"So, begin," the old man urged.

From memory, Robbie spoke in Hebrew. "And when her days to be delivered were fulfilled, behold, there were twins in her womb.

"And the first came out red all over like a hairy garment; and they called his name Esau," Robbie recited.

"And after came his brother out, his hand holding onto Esau's heel . . ." Together into the darkness their voices took up the ancient legend. "And Jacob rose up early in the morning, and took the stone that he had put for his pillow and set it up for a pillar," the old man continued the tale.

"And this stone which I have set for a pillar shall be God's house; and of all that thou wilt give me I will surely give the tenth unto thee," Robbie ended.

Robbie closed his eyes on the stone pillow of Lazar Fein's small bed, at peace in the sanctuary of the sexton's house.

There would be honey cake and wine and the guest list would include only his grandmother and aunt, his mother and father. His parents had shrugged at the neighbors' surprise, blamed orthodoxy's simple demands. "Well, it certainly pays to be pious," Aunt Elaine sought consolation, deprived of the ardor of the reception plans.

No fittings, gowns, music. No photographer, caterer. The suit need not be the finest, for, as Grandma Goldschmitt sighed, "Who'll know?" Robbie took himself from the swirl of talk, the phone calls to the women on his mother's side.

"Hate to interrupt your—uh—studies," his father shifted from one foot to another, standing inside Robbie's door, startling him with the gentleness of tone.

"Looks like a cell around here. A monastery or some-thing." His father laughed uneasily, waving to walls bare of pennants, snapshots, pictures of the school soccer team. Boxed, too, were the beer-can bank Natie had given him, the naked-lady lamp, the *National Lampoons* his brother had left behind. His father shifted weight again, holding out a velvet pouch like an offering.

"Robbie," he cleared his throat. "Will this be okay with Fein? My bar mitzvah *tallis*. Natie wore it, and if it is good enough . . ." Nowhere could Robbie recall tales of his father's bar mitzvah ritual. What meaning had it had? His father would need the shawl at least once again, to be wrapped for death. Taking its silky length, he let the fringe flutter against the blue velvet, embossed with lions on a crown.

In the front pew of the tiny *shul*, Robbie sat now with his cronies. Face after face—Morris, Stein, Krokowitz, Pinsky, Pulsky, Mandelbaum—reflected the fire newly kindled. They rose, mourners all, to evoke the memory of their departed, as fresh as a new-turned grave, for only that week had they buried one of their lingering few.

By him sat his father. Never did a man look less fitted to a prayer garment—property of Beth Elohim. Even the skull-cap seemed to slip dangerously from his bullish head. When his name was called, he rose to read his passage in transliteration. An imperceptible shrug flitted across his shoulders as he took his seat, a retort to the accusation of Beth Elohim.

In the woman's loft sat his mother and aunt and grandmother. How beautiful his mother looked, the blonde curls sprung from their rollers, framing her smiling face. Fein had explained it was the custom for the sexes to be separate, the women's charms safely boxed away. How else can men's minds be pure in hallowed places! His mother's eyes roamed the congregation and settled at last upon her younger son. He winked shyly back, wishing she were by his side.

He didn't feel like a man! Thirteen! *Was* that the end of childhood? How long was it, really, to be a boy? He would step forward when his name was called and belong to all the boys who had come before him.

Robbie looked at Reb Fein, being assisted in the opening of the ark by the old men. From them he had taken the teachings, a resting spot, these weeks, to slip quietly from being a boy to the man he was becoming. He would miss the old *shul*. The dusty afternoons. His friends. His mother understood. Would his father let him return, stay on still for Sabbath eves? Some day, when he was a man, a real man, he would come back to this congregation—would it be here still?—where being Jewish had begun.

Now Robbie heard the rabbi call his Hebrew name, Reuvain ben Avram.

His teacher spread his hands above Robbie's bowed head.

"May the Lord bless thee and keep thee. May the Lord shine His countenance upon thee," he intoned, "and grant thee peace."

Wholly covered by his prayer cloths, wholly stooped in the manner of his mentors, he kept from tripping on his fringe. Swaddled thus, Robbie bent at last to the scrolls. His tenor rang in purest style.

# WHERE TOUCHING IS A TALENT

———

When he finally fell asleep, the dawn blended with the ballroom lights and music that wove themselves into his dreams. Eight hours Leo had spent in its oasis, the Thursdays of his life, secret Thursday, Leo's magical day. Every Thursday the salesman pleaded to be let out of work early. "Meeting the wife for dinner, you know how it is." Mr. Frankland his boss didn't know. He only knew Leo racked up enough sales every Thursday by four to earn the time off. So then Leo would cross the twelve city blocks faster than it took to find shoes in the stacks. Leo would wave, wink, tip his hat to strange women brushing past, a man warming for flesh that waited in a dance hall at the end of the quick stroll.

All these dancing years, what fibs he sold Sophie: overtime without fatter pay, a horror movie she would have hated, the age-old "sick friend" routine, older than friendships themselves. If only Sophie cared or noticed. Did she mark the powerful mint burying the nip of liquor, taken merely to wet his whistle? Or the lateness of his postmidnight tiptoe home? Moving over, opening to his return, she gave no sign. Leo rocked then to the music in his head, gliding above his sleeping wife. She sighed, stirred. Soft moans sprung from the shallow life beating still beneath her ribs. He blew lightly on her nipples but her breasts never rose to the lift of his groin. Leo spit on his hand, moistened her, and slipped, slipped to darkened partings, sure of his grace, a cadent slide. "Baby, baby," Leo whispered, exalting with each stroke,

39

taking the lost woman after the late Thursdays, after the eight-hour Thursday dance.

"Hey, Lee, boy, put it there!" With hands on hands, slaps on backs and growing ten feet tall, Leo would make his entrance. At Roseland, doors swung open and Leo felt the red sea part. All those strangers rushing down city streets, soon as step over you. But not in Leo's mecca, his club, his parlor, his home. Tinsel and flicker and lights and roses strewn on acres of carpets, the winding stairways he skipped without touching a rail. The ticket taker and wardrobe mistress, the checkroom boy, the bartender, the pro who taught amateurs but could learn a thing from him—all of them greeted Leo with pressed flesh, touching, touching, in the only haven where touching was a talent, where tenderness flourished on a polished floor. Dancing, guiding some lovely, Leo's heart filled all its empty spaces. All week he would wait for the backslaps and handshakes of the men, the slipping toward his waist and legs and arms of scented women.

Leo had learned young to depend on minor senses. Smell was the first, saluting the rank rooms his family fled from or toward. Stored in the memories of childhood was the peculiar odor of each. Now Leo trusted scent as much to judge the essence of things as hearing, touch, and sight, the cries of all his senses all of his bent week. At Roseland that air was of sweat and smoke, pomade and shoe polish, rosin that slicked the floors, and over it all, perfumes that grew with body heat. All this brewed in Leo's head and hit him fresh each week. Never in any public place sought thereafter was he met by the special aroma of dance hall.

Beneath street level, a serf could be a prince or princess. Dusting powder and Mum and Colgate emerged from little cases carried from their jobs, a redolence lingering behind dressing room doors, shutting off their daytime life. Leo took his turn at the tinted oval mirrors, swagged in plaster above mottled marble shelves. He flexed his shoulders and muscles, tightened his abdomen, checked his tongue for white, flossed the gold fillings. Beside him some old hoofer penciled youth to whitened temples. Leo smiled at the withered dancer with a rush of pity.

Presiding over all this nether establishment was the arthritic madam, Bettina, wardrobe mistress supreme, née Betty Carmichael of Coney Island. Her golden slippers hung now on a peg next to tea-colored news clips which extended the boast of the shoes. Leo slipped his hand furtively inside her dress. Bettina loved it! She guided it toward her flat plates, called him fresh, giggled. He kissed her wrinkled neck. Where would his own shoes hang when his dancing days were done?

The shiny slippers rested in rows of boxes Bettina held for regulars. Some gathered dust while their owners recuperated from illness or surgery or the deaths of their beloved. The dustiest belonged to the boys in service. Some day they'd return, if they still had legs to dance with, and take them down again for still another spin.

There in the city-block basement, the wardrobe lady also stored the dancing dresses, the petticoats that kept the skirts' bell shape, saving them with wrappers, robes, or cellophane. Bettina need not tag them, for their owners could be her children, as remembered and as doted on.

Nor were there, across the way, checkroom tags. Such mystery, these underground workings. All day Leo carried in his head numbers, the numbers of sizes and colors and styles. But here, at the checkroom, purses and possessions were left and never a tag changed hands. Like at a speakeasy, the keeper whispered a number, remembered all of the whirling hours to be called up for redemption when it was time to leave. No dancer need carry to the floor the burden of even a tiny card.

With a final glance to the mirror, Leo approved his role change. He gazed at his image, looking past it to the one waiting at home. "There was this monster, hon, one-eyed, hunchback, claws instead of hands and fangs instead of a tongue." Rocking before the morning window, Sophie would appear to nod. But Leo was never sure. A quiet woman was what he wanted. Silence was what he got, the stillness of a grave. In those long-gone early years of marriage, Leo had been powerless to hold his wife, all life itself, from ebbing away.

Sophie new! Yes, even the sere and brittle begin with promise and juices flowing. It was '35 then, a never-never time before war, and Sophie, imp, had given the salesman a run for it. When had Leo worked so hard in all his two dozen years! Sophie didn't walk, she bounced. He'd watched her move down the street of shops, he standing before the shoe store, wishing for something good. The girl darted in and out, grinning delight when an item held her. His gaze rose from her sturdy oxfords to the sensible shirtwaist, denied by the fresh daisy tucked in black, straight-falling hair.

When he bent to undo her laces, a nip of lemon flew from hidden sources. Thick lisle kept the secret of her legs. But Leo felt the spring of elastic calves and flawless feet.

Her voice held a tease, as she changed from one pair to another. "Looks like we'll never agree on what's right for me," she faked an exaggerated sigh, a game both players understood. How he longed to balance the sprite upon his hand. Instead, as surprised as she to hear it, he blurted, "Come dancing tonight! I'm free if you are!"

The something good did happen. Sophie could dance, oh could she! She leaned her head on Leo's shoulder and talked only when Leo wanted (oh, if every girl knew that secret) and never while dancing, as reverent as in temple. A scented hanky soaked up the sweat of their palms and her breath was Wrigley's sweet. She didn't request drinks in the middle of a set. When Leo led her into intricate grapevines, Sophie swiftly followed and never needed to sit out the fast or syncopated beats.

Later, only minutes later, the band stroking them with smoky echoes, "Goodnight, sweetheart, parting is such sorrooowww . . .," the couple held their twine all the way to the changing room below.

Sophie let Leo wind the ribbons high above her ankle, but stopped him at her door. "Can I kiss you good night?" Leo breathed. "I'd rather not," she whispered. "I'd rather," Leo whispered back.

Sophie nearly danced down the aisle of the tiny synagogue in spite of her parents' hold on either arm. Leo's parents marched him down, too, each pair of sponsors bestowing their treasure upon the other. And Sophie, ah Sophie, weightless, pert, airy, and full of grace, rested in Leo's arms not more than two good years.

The fine ballroom form translated to the bed. Here Sophie moved to a baton even more compelling. Too modest to accept its joy, she longed for its quick return. Jews committed to progeny, they trusted to nightly joinings to bring results.

Young and impatient at those first fruitless months, Sophie told Leo, "If I rest more, maybe it'll take." Resting meant sleeping late, dressing little, even dropping dancing, as though that was ever work! Resting meant being ripe for Leo at dawn and ready again at night. But as the woman felt herself a vessel only for transient visits, her spirit ran out with her monthly flow.

Tonight Stan Roberts, the smaller half of the management team, was grabbing Leo, keeping him from the floor. "Hey, Lee-boy, hear the latest, the one about the Nazi doctor giving the Jerry an aspirin? 'Put vun unter your *dong* effrey two hours!' Ya get it, Leo-baby? Under your tongue. *Dong!* Ha, ha," nudging Leo's balls. It was 1942 and the war, no joke, was all the jokes.

How Stan's shoes dazzled by Leo's feet, reflecting the lights bouncing off them. Didn't nuns warn girls off patent leather? White Catholic faces came to him, schoolgirls in blue jumpers, prim upon his sizing scale.

Before permitting himself to a partner, Leo stood in the

shadows, ringside. He appraised the upholstered chairs
where the women of his Thursdays waited.

Leona MacGuiness, chugging with fellow stenos every
week from Philly, two hours by train and back. In the home
of brotherly love, was there no really snappy stepper?
Pinched, knock-kneed beneath a heaving prow of hips, how
Leona spread those flashy legs.

Eva, her stately fox-trot a standout among the newer,
swingier moves. Cameo dangling from velvet choker, spit
curls high, Eva could be in some iridescent painting. Leo had
once seen a Met poster in the subway, ladies under parasols
by the sea, all of it in polka dots. Eva moved that way, one
black-lace glove barely touching the lead, scarlet chiffoning
from its mate.

There was The Doc, the Park Ave. lady shrink, shedding
Peck 'n Pecks for siren reds. And the courtly Viennese
couple, refugees from Hitler's evil! And a bimbo in drag,
risking Stan and Dan, the Tweedledee and Tweedledum who
upheld the dance hall's class. Near the bandstand Leo picked
out Baroness Esmerelda, whose secret title he'd keep if
tortured. He waved here and there to housewives presumed
at bridge, mah-jongg, or bingo. (Marriage held no openings
for the dance.) He searched for his pal Randall, the blind
piano tuner, led to the floor by his dog. How the gals were
quick to take over, quickened to his step. In a dark corner
were a boxer and a football pro he recognized, developing
fast footwork, their fans should only know, and in the center,
a couple of dance masters being rented out by their rich and
lonely pupils.

Like medals on a suit, the uniforms of the brave armed
forces flashed adventure to the locals: Tango Jack and Rag-
time Willy and Rosa-named-for-Roseland and Manuel the
Cuban Romeo; Sadie the Dancing Lady, Loolu, Mehitabel,
Rosalinda; women whose names might be Martha or Mary
or Margaret in daylight; all of whom Leo sought among the
shadows or flitting between the beams. No bombs or battles
had taken this last home-front refuge. Nothing was changed.

Venerable and stable, Roseland was an anchor, an island, the only warmth of the cold and rushing city.

He begged Sophie to consider war work. Good for you, baby, build your morale. Everywhere morale was being offered: to defense workers, to our boys overseas, to the home front bravely waiting. If Sophie couldn't be a welder, she could at least fold bandages, fill in somewhere for an able-bodied male.

Morale was what Sophie lacked the most. Morale was what Sophie needed even before Pearl Harbor burned. How could she pass the days, blending one into another, living for Stella Dallas, Our Gal Sunday, Helen Trent, letting radio people take the place of real ones! Leo went from his folks to hers, imploring them of her need. But Leo's mother went on chopping, Sophie's playing solitaire. As though loose lips would sink ships. A conspiracy of silence.

As he did now every week, Leo searched for The Jap, though these days she called herself Korean. The Jap was the best of his possibilities. With MacArthur sending her most honorable ones to hari-kari, she shared with him her parents' grief. She told Leo of her Irish-German husband, rich on ration books, the Bronx butcher who believed her Thursdays were for a sick aunt. These and other secrets The Jap whispered to Leo over mint-masked drinks, filling in the six days between each week. But Leo never shared with The Jap his Sophie, the girl he had once waltzed into his hungry life.

Sophie's pregnancy, at last, had begun with unleashed vomiting, rushing Leo toward Mount Sinai's I.V. The color died on Sophie's cheeks and her figure never bloomed. She grew thinner every month. "You'll see," he cheered her. "At the end you'll be bursting with that kid of mine." But at the end Sophie had gained a mere eight pounds. Toxemia swelled her legs and little swelled her stomach. Blue welts began a fine tracery on her legs—the dancing legs!—receding only when Sophie rested them upon a chair. Everything that had pointed up, breasts, nose, chin, was drawn downward by the coming child.

The blood loss of the delivery had made it touch and go, draining even more of Sophie's weight. Yet Laurinda, as fine as any name taken by a dancer, bellowed into the world with a lusty cry from a body healthy, round, and pink.

"She's gorgeous," Leo bubbled to the mother, whose glucose still dripped rhythmically above her. When Sophie's breasts yielded little, the doctor removed the infant from her nipples and onto canned milk.

"Laurinda, Lauri, Laurene," Leo played with the name, oblivious to faces pressing the nursery window. He swung into little routines, whirling the obese desk nurse to a soundless ditty.

Hey there, kiddo, I'll be your teacher. Shirley Temple, move over! Laurinda would have the pep for any partner, move through every figure, for there she was, thriving in her bassinet, waving arms for immediate attention, as bold a howler as any of the infants wrapped like blintzes in their blankets. Leo and his parents and his in-laws came to the hospital twice a day, devoted to the gift behind glass, overlooking the donor pinned to a bottle in a nearby room.

For the 1943 Harvest Moon Ball, Leo decided he and The Jap should take new names. His partner wasn't very clever, so Leo read Chinese menus till he came up with something inscrutable. Lo-Li and Lee Monty! Six weeks, only six weeks to practice before Madison Square Garden and the *Daily News* brought the best bands and feet together. The trophies and prizes were wilder than ever, to up the annual draw.

"You know how it is, Mr. Frankland. The sick wife. Needs me at home." And Mr. Frankland didn't know how it is and didn't like it a bit that Leo took all of Thursday afternoons off. It was the beginning of the school-shoes season and couldn't the sick wife pick an easier time to drag the salesman away?

Leo practically ran then between stockroom and customer,

doubling sales. And practically ran at noon to Roseland and The Jap, where for the next four hours, before the crowd drifted in, they had more of the polished maple. All of the waning hours they honed the little running steps, switching to artful broad strides. Curled under his arm again and again, twirling in dizzying pivots, The Jap, ah the breath control of these Asians, never panted.

She was fashioning a Kabuki gown and would wind her hair like a geisha wig. A makeup artist had agreed to paint her as a doll. She did not sweat, The Jap assured Leo, and would not greet the judges with a runny face. Leo schemed to brandish a samurai sword for their entrance, tie her to his wrist, and cut her away with its blade!

A quickening spread toward Leo's guts. The prize, a thousand smackers, more than the Thursday commissions of the next ten years! A thousand bucks for his daughter's books, college, good shoes. And the glory, the glory! Sayonara, Mr. Frankland. Stuff your fucking shoes!

Now when Leo returned from the late Thursdays, he went first to the wicker bassinet in the corner of their tiny bedroom, greeted by uric-tainted talc, dried milk on bibs, clean piled wrappers, the rubber of the crib mat, and the Ivory Soap of crib sheets, making this the most aromatic of all of Leo's homes.

Sophie had draped the infant's bed with gauze, shrouding her with the mystery of Scheherazade. A stuffed animal in each corner stood guard. Leo bent to the infant, her fist to her mouth as if to suck all the clenched fingers at once. Let others settle for a mere thumb!

"Hey, Beautiful," Leo whispered. "Getting prettier every day for Daddy?" Leo lifted the tucked-in blanket gently and fondled each of his daughter's tucked-in feet, rounded for sleep under a humped tush. A baby's foot had no ankle, a mere flower at the tip of a curled stalk. Leo, breathing on each, nipping the toes lovingly, running a broad tongue across the insteps, cherished the precious feet. She stirred at his wetness, settled back to infant dreams, and Leo stripped in the dark, caressing himself largely, before giving his remaining affection to his wife.

What a draw, such a draw! The best ever! Fans and dancers and rooters filling to the top the rows of seats. The bands as dazzling in their attire as in their beat. All of the Roseland regulars scrambling in, the management closing its doors to the public for that one spangled night. As the emcee boomed into the mike each of the stage names of the contesting couples, wild cheers rang out in their behalf.

Bettina and the Tweedle-bouncers and the bartender and the checkroom attendants, the dance pros who gave the weekly free lessons, as well as the studio pros who paraded their prize pupils around Roseland's mirrored floor, families and friends and backers who'd put up good money to outfit a particular pair and would split the winnings if there were some, the nondancer looking for an evening's entertainment and the would-be dancer wistfully living vicariously, all these clambered up and up into the outer reaches of that arena. Who would believe a mere dance spectacle could merit such a crush?

For weeks the *News* had run pictures of past winners and headless shots of the picked favorites. Provocative bodies and whipping feet, the photos were intended not to bias the judges but to titillate the fans. Everyone who was savvy knew, of course, the Waltzing Mat and Matilda, the Charles and Charlene of the Mean-Mean Charleston, and more, and more.

Over the years there had been Hawaiians and Indians, of both American and far-off persuasion. Dancers gotten up as circus acts or lion tamers, and oh, every manner of gimmick. The Old Smoothies in sedate tails and wispy trails were staples, and from time to time someone innovated in black-face, taking off on minstrels, or donned patches to simulate hoboes.

The announcer's voice echoed and re-echoed, rebounding

along the rafters. The band struck up a flourish. "Tonight, a first! The Samurai Steppers in an Asian tango, Lee Monty and Lo-Li, the Lightning Duo of the East!"

Blind. Stinko. Blotto. Head-reeling, speech-slurring, feet-slipping drunk. Leo's sword, bent beyond its swath, tapped a tattoo upon every hydrant. He sang, "Can't give you anyshing but looove, babee," ignoring windows raised in anger, cans aimed for his head.

He'd taken the little Jap to the subway, he was sure. "No hari-kari, ya hear?" he joked away her tears. Na, he wouldn't need the subway himself. Walking's good for the feet, good exercise. Ha, ha! What these feet needed, a little workout.

Leo talked to the feet that had let him down.

"What good are friends when ya need 'em and they won't do their stuff?" It was a very serious lecture. He sat by the edge of the road and fastidiously ejected a bile vomit. "Shee, Shophie, gonna have a baby! Ha, ha, little joke," he sobbed. He began to wipe the mess with a huge hanky, but changed his mind and left it to cover the slop. "Neatness counts," he remembered from somewhere long ago.

Putting the key in was impossible. He aimed it with both hands but it wavered before the hole. Maybe he'd sleep in the building's hall, a professional drunk! Bum! Mamma would call him *mumser,* lowlife, schmuck, Mamma who served seltzer when schnapps was called for. "Shorry, Mamma, Shophie," he whispered, bowing again to the keyhole. "I losht, losht. Your Leo'sh a losher, Mamma!" the dancer wept.

Finally the key clicked in its latch. Leo tiptoed to the bedroom and stashed the dancing slippers down, down into the hamper. In his socks he leaned toward his daughter's heat. He took her curled finger in his. Cold! Icy as polished glass. Leo shook his head to clear it. Filthy drunkard! He lifted Laurinda, wrapping her tightly to warm her. Why was she so cold? He hugged her in one arm and with the other pumped the old Victrola. He groped for a record, too dark to read its label. Gently he slid the needle into the groove, the bunting finally lifting from his brain. "Come and be my melancholy bayy beee," Crosby groaned. Lightly, lightly, Leo and Laurinda danced in the blackness, the baby cold upon his heaving heart.

# EQUATIONS

Twelve years was long enough to wait to marry Cornelius. Every spring for the first few years the teachers threw the usual bridal shower, but now even they had given up. Twelve years of starting a diet every March for fittings every May for postponements every June. How they snickered, the ingenues, deflowered first, ringed later, and gone away with child before the next term's end.

About the tenth year of her engagement, Renie noticed a change. Like a dog trained to heel at a glance, her figure held its weight, could hold for Cornelius forever, sparing her at least that prenuptial detail. Her trousseau saw her through every vagary of fashion, from mini to midcalf to midknee. While Cornelius read travel brochures and real estate ads, vacillated betweeen the horoscope and the weather report, she kept the dresses in their plastic, the hems going up and down with her hopes.

How Cornelius dazzled her with his wisecracks and impressed her with his prudence. In their apartment, as far from Mother as across the street, it was she who made the judgments. He would tease her into rash decisions and invalidate every one. But Cornelius, balancing his Libra against her Scorpio, had of course been smart to wait. It was only when the engagement ring, bought twelve years ago when she was full—full of figure and full of promise—dropped through the drain in the sink, that Renie let herself slip from its noose. For the first time in twelve years she made a firm decision.

She told Cornelius to go to hell.

* * *

How strange to wake with no Cornelius by her side, nor soon to be dropping in. All the betrothal years, sharing him with Mother, cooking for three, all the long evenings of TV and Triple Yahtzee, how much space he was meant to fill. Renie stretched her arm against the cornflower sheets, recalling his rump and rumble. Cornelius, intended to complete herself, good for an evening's breeze, mere bluster when it meant being wedded down. She rose and studied the full-length mirror, glad for the steady slimness. Her eyes, grayer than the bed's flowers, stared from deep-set rims. She filled a mug that matched fiesta mats. Across their weeks of silent coffee, every sip had been a gulp for breath. Had Cornelius sucked all the air with his endless planning while the present waited to be grasped at last?

The windows of her apartment faced Mother's. Raising the shade seemed to trigger the phone each morning. Now Renie steeled herself from Mother. No, she didn't mind being alone, wouldn't "come home." Renie agreed to see her at fixed times and planned to stop raising the shade.

Renie weighed herself. Obedient dog. She would buy a handsome different kind of wardrobe, velours, velvets, and glossy silks to light her path into the singles world. New power would propel her toward new decisions, help her decide where to take out her fine clothing, let decisions become a habit. Didn't confidence reach for the confidence of others? Then she, too, would be caught in the energy field that was love and know what heroines of novels knew. She would let positive thinking fill her dreams.

The teachers' room buzz simmered down when Renie crossed its threshold. Teacher talk—sales, restaurants, dates—always needed something more. Renie Dugan gave it that extra for twelve years. Miss Dugan was accustomed to setting off tongues.

"Single, single, and always to remain so," they had scoffed. Single, yes. But now by choice.

Auditing the teachers' room, Renie pretended to correct

papers. "Copley's," they said. For the up-and-coming, the if-not-yets, the surely promising.

"You sit at the bar," they said, "and sooner than later someone strikes up a conversation." When a male teacher dropped in, the talk switched in midbreath, leaving Renie somewhere between the canny and the conned.

"Copley's," Renie penciled lightly on the corner of Randy Sullivan's spelling test.

The decision to visit the singles' bar was all day coming. The one to go braless took longer. Abandoning its support, she patted furtively, a self-exam for respectability. No. Renie returned to the bedroom and gathered her drooping sacs, raisin-nubbed, into their wires. She slid a shimmer of low-cut dress over the braces. Extra eye shadow, shimmery too.

But out in the gusts whipping the city's litter, Renie felt her bosom again. At Copley's might a male elbow brush against her? Renie returned to her building and rode the elevator back up to the apartment. In the dark, she reached inside her dress, unsnapped the front fastener, breathed, and slipped the bra from under.

At Copley's, Sammy's piano jazz cushioned the nervous talk. For forty minutes Renie nuzzled her margarita. The bartender kept throwing her looks suggesting she was overparked. Renie smiled brightly when an up-and-coming seemed to approach. Behind the women seated on high stools, leering men sidled. The mirrored bar reflected their little knots of twosomes. When she had been a tiny girl on the flying horses, her father had stood behind her to keep her from falling. Now she held her balance, gave the margarita another twenty minutes to disappear, and disappeared herself down the dimly lighted street.

Renie signed up for a dance course, A Party At Every Lesson. Two dance masters, Mr. M. and Mr. W., took turns with eight women, while the six leftovers threw knives at each other waiting out the dance. Mr. M. exuded garlic, Mr. W.

booze. Renie let them finger the notches on her spine as if it were an intricate keyboard. Mr. W. placed his hand on her hip, moving it to her thigh for the tango. Her neck hung over his shoulder. When Renie returned to the little iron table to watch Mr. W. stride the other women through their tango, she saw him use the edge of a matchbook to pick his teeth.

The next evening Renie invited Mother to dinner. She would compare notes with the widow of three decades now that she too was a woman alone. But Mother chattered about daytime serials, making Renie feel less than half a person. When Mother went home, the missing parts returned. Is this what being *one* is, alone, steering one's own ship? It was a comforting notion, being a navigator, her class a sort of crew. But the cornflowers stretched away from her and she tossed on waves of blossoms where the vessels had no captains, all of them unguided, none drifting toward her lonely wake.

"A good mind in a good body," Renie wrote on the board. "A stitch in time" no longer spoke to today's pupils. It was all health, nutrition, organic, bionic. She looked out upon her eager crew, heads bent, chewing pencils, ballpoints clicking with their minds. "Youth is truth," she wanted to write. Youth is muscles and high jumps and Rumanian Nadias. Only a gym teacher reached a modern child.

Waldo Rogers had taught phys ed since the time he was built for it. His was a swagger the young teachers mocked. An older teacher might call it confidence. Holding the door for her, maneuvering her auto out of tight parking spots, toting her briefcase, the gym teacher gave Renie status among her pupils. One Monday afternoon the gym teacher also gave her a weekend date.

All week Renie hurried the days away. She pushed her basket through the market, hearing the Muzak for the first time. One-two-three-four, lunging the basket ahead of her. Around the cart a small twirl, dipping toward the bottom shelf in time to the music. Two-three-four, into the cart with the noodles. Renie led a mop into the next number, but catching sight of an approaching white apron, threw it back against the wall.

After school on Friday, Renie leaned back against the bucket of Waldo's jaunty Toyota, up and up through Mount Washington's winding rise, floating in Waldo's mentholated smoke. Later, in the motel, Waldo crooned, "I love ya, honey, love ya," rocking above her. He was shorter than Cornelius, shorter than Renie, panting at her shoulders, giving her the sensation of a dog having his way. Asleep at once, he required a shove aside, where he snored heavily all of the untouched night. "Love ya," he told her again as they packed to leave.

Renie smoothed the unworn robe in her case, rolled the toothpaste tube another notch, tucked it with her brush. Waldo tossed pajamas to his overnighter on the chair. He threw both their cases under his arm and headed for the car. Back he came with another larger piece of luggage, flinging it empty upon the bed. Reached to the closet shelf, removing the extra blanket. Sprinted to the bathroom, and whistling "Oh What a Beautiful Morning," scooped up all the towels.

Renie hung a sweater on her shaking frame.

Two drinking glasses slipped to Waldo's luggage. Renie gasped in frozen horror. Into the suitcase Waldo stuffed the pillow. Fist to mouth, Renie fled to the car.

Alone at home that night, she selected one of her sheer black trousseau nightgowns. She tuned the radio to soft dance music and lit a scented candle. Hugging a bed pillow in the dim glow, Renie pulsed to whatever the radio ordered.

The "Calendar" section of the Thursday paper was the teachers' bible. It ran the week's events, and under "People" was the list for singles. Dancing ranged from ballroom to contra. The music at coffeehouses was both folk and jazz. There was group cross-country, backgammon, and Scrabble. Renie studied the offerings and circled the most promising.

At the Weekend Brunch Club, men and women hovered

over the buffet. Stuffed eggs vied with the bagels. When Renie had phoned for information, the entrepreneur explained the brunch's potluck nature. Now with each bruncher split between the nourishment and the potential, clearly the mating was potluck too.

Only one woman and one man circulated with ease, confident in their eye contact, comfortable in their clothes. As this Mr. Wonderful neared, Renie's throat closed over her deviled egg. She envied his sureness. Should she offer him her hand, already juggling napkin and mug?

"I'm Renie Dugan, a teacher," she blurted.

"And I'm Dr. Proctovsky, behavioral psychologist," he said, touching her shoulder, ignoring her hand. "You get me for the speaker after the food." He beamed, a lighthouse in a storm. His smiling counterpart, Renie suddenly realized, was surely Mrs. Proctovsky, buttressing his role. Of course they were relaxed. They were the only guests certain to leave partnered.

On Tuesday it was the library. With obsolescence driving it to offer more, its bulletin board proclaimed courses, lectures, poetry readings, films. The weekly discussion of Short American Novels seemed to Renie not too heavy, not too light. Not notably for singles, no one came for touching. But similar to singles' groups, only first names were scrawled on bright sticky tags.

Bob, denim overalled in sharp contrast to the aging students, distributed the review questions. "Interior experience? Intrinsic motivation? Interwoven subplots?" Who said fiction was frivolous escape!

On Wednesday Renie was pushed by the crush to the doors of Symphony Hall, the crowd as tensely poised for their opening as at some rock concert. Wondering why people clutched extra wraps, Renie eavesdropped on their strategies. In pairs or clusters, some were to run to grab space for the prerehearsal lecture, while others were deployed to toss coats on unreserved seats. Guerrilla warfare extended survival at

Open Rehearsals the way she and Mother organized assaults on Filene's Basement, where it was also good to have a team.

Elbow to Renie's elbow was a portly gent, bereted and bearded. Surprised at her courage, she asked the stranger to save her a seat while she made the dash to the lecture hall. He agreed in European accents certain to be academic. He was passing up the lecture, but he'd hold seats by the aisle, front center. Would that do?

How smooth the transaction! None of the uneasy footwork of other first encounters. When the doors were finally flung wide, the wolves attacked. In the hall, the musicologist played themes on the piano and chatted about the program, his listeners savoring every word.

At lecture's end, Renie went with the flow into the concert hall. There, the European professor hailed her. Renie's heart beat and her joy leaped. How easy it was to meet a good man here. The teachers and their singles life! But now he was introducing her to a woman by his side.

"My wife, a violinist, was teaching and could come only now." Straight blonde American hair fell from a face not yet twenty-five, young enough to be his daughter. Ah, Renie thought, youth is truth.

Blue-jeaned and sweatered, the orchestra feigned a sporting event, their casualness belying their famed precision. Now, to the applause of rising players and rising audience, a small Asian leaped to the podium. The instruments were lifted and Mahler's mournful notes crept in. "The Resurrection" swelled. The conductor opened his arms to the music, a dancer with a baton. Why, not even Nureyev had such grace. Swaying and bowing, he ordered the air with a curled caress.

To Renie there was no one, no riveted audience, no musicians, nothing but this taut energy. She closed her eyes, swaying with him. She danced the scherzo in her head, felt the maestro's hands upon her, drawing music from her locked loins.

One Sunday Renie watched a wedding party throng to a

nearby hotel. Ten bridesmaids! A garden of pastels! They chattered like crystal all the way indoors. Distinguished parents alighted from the limousine. Their temples were as gray-tipped as if ordered there by Bachrach. Peering above the gathering crowd, Renie waited for the bridal couple. At last they too disembarked. The groom bent sturdily to help his bride's train. The bride, why the bride was a mere glowing child. Renie shivered, wrapping round her a dozen years.

Sweeping hands over angular hips, breasts free of bras forever, she followed the party into the glittering hall. Admitting to neither the bride's nor the groom's side, Renie moved through the receiving line. "Congratulations, congratulations," she whispered. The faces smiled back, but tension passed from every hand she squeezed.

She stood at the bar, mingled with the guests, nibbled the hors d'oeuvres. A young man helped her to the caviar, smiling, energy-charged. Renie picked it up on her own magnetic field.

"The bride's never looked lovelier, has she?" Renie began on an up note, but the guest, an out-of-towner, had never met the bride.

"Oh she's sort of the intellectual type," Renie explained.

"Well, I hope you're not!" the man laughed.

Renie moved on to a ruddy gentleman juggling two hot pigs-in-blankets. "Good to see you again, Martha!" he hailed her, choking with a full mouth. With her confidence spreading, Renie shook hands, alive to the long-lost "relatives." Repartee came to her and lambent wit. She darted in and out among them like a hummingbird and, when the band struck up, was an easy partner to someone's cousin.

This was the pattern of her days: weekly dinners with Mother, dancing to the radio, the evening capped with one of the library's good books. Weddings nearly every Sunday. Sundays were her secret to look back upon all week, the flowers and music and brides, especially the brides. Satisfaction seeped toward her heart.

At night she'd wonder about those united couples. Since Sunday School and Noah's Ark, she had trusted the unity of marriage. But *could* you give yourself to another and yet keep what you had? Caring for another, a man, could she retain her *ownness,* so new and warm and fine?

Miss Dugan's third grade was cited for model behavior. The medal signifying it graced her corkboard. Although some years were better than others, was there ever a class who seemed so glad to get her teaching? Tutoring Sally Gorman one afternoon, Renie smiled at the girl's pensive struggle. The sun's rays slanted toward the dusty chalkboard and across the child's solemn face. When the lesson was over, Sally suddenly hugged the teacher across her skirt, stammering "Beautiful lady!" and dashing shyly out.

Each student reached toward Renie in a way that felt new. "Individualization" was this year's catchword, yet another of education's unattainables. Renie tried harder to fulfill that goal. She tried to make classwork relevant. She improvised spelling assignments around current school events. Math simulated actual experiences. When Randy's collie had four pups, she put on the board:

$$\frac{4 \text{ pups}}{X} = \text{?}$$

She wrote: If Randy has four pups and one dog, and it costs four dollars a week to feed a full-grown collie, how much will it cost the Sullivans a year to feed five adult dogs? She was teaching not only math but also pet responsibility.

Toward the end of the school year, Renie noticed sudden new topics in the teachers' room. As partnering had been the favorite, now split-ups were as popular. Divorce, widowhood, who was available, left out, or left behind. It, too, could be a math problem, the remainder carried to its second decimal point.

Worst among them, Renie saw, were the smugly married. Evil roamed the world, dividing from the faithful their philandering mates, subtracting from the devoted their failing spouses. Were they not worried, these wedded ones, given today's odds?

Mother talked of widowhood, never its cause. When she'd prattle about her desertion, Renie tried to fix upon the culprit. But Father stopped at her childhood, when he'd dropped in dead surprise. All she remembered were doors closing on a rushing figure and Mother forever alone, buried in loneness. Renie let the woman go on and on about daytime TV, her vicarious media friends, but Renie never shared her own vicarious Sundays.

Lately parent conferences were dotted with fathers. One, a custody victor, another the victim of desertion, listened meekly and hastened from her as soon as they politely could. When Sally's mother was struck by a drunk driver, the widower sent Sally's grandmother in his place.

Renie worried about these pupils' lives. Now when she finished reading the marriage intentions, finished calculating Sunday's wedding, she flipped through the paper to the obituaries. She unraveled the journalism jargon.

"Died suddenly." Possibly heart.

"Found dead." Suicide.

"After a lingering illness." Probably cancer.

Renie imagined the lingering grief. Husbands hungry for comfort. Families motherless long before mother was gone. To Renie, obituaries were novels not yet written. She tried to picture the bereaved, letting the names roll on her tongue. What majesty was given to the language of these columns. "Prominent in the community." "Lifetime resident." "Long in public service." She savored "pallbearers" and "honorary pallbearers." Too bizarre for this week's vocabulary list? She reflected on whom the "deceased" had left behind. When the "demise" what that of a young woman, Renie could see "Tracy" or "Jodie" or "Kim" lighting candles "in memoriam." She longed to balm their innocence.

Renie heated milk and butter, the best sleeping pill in the world. She gave her teeth twenty strokes and her hair fifty lashes. Propping her book upon her chest, she read till her eyes could hold no longer. The tale wove itself into her dreams and in the morning she did not know which was literature and which her own dark hopes.

When she'd read *Seize the Day,* she could not drop off. Its antihero haunted her turns and tosses. "The flowers and lights fused ecstatically in Wilhelm's blind wet eyes; the heavy sea-like music came up . . ." In the end the day had been seized at a stranger's funeral. What better refuge for a mourner of life itself?

The very next Saturday, Renie took to the literary example. She plucked from her closet a banker's gray suit. As she straightened the stock-tied shirt, the glass reflected her assurance. The long walk to the funeral parlor blew her hair into a nimbus, put color to her skin. She followed the small group into the dimness of the chapel, gathering the serenity to her.

Shedding the anonymity she wore at the alien nuptials, she put her name to the undertaker's register. She slipped to the pew and bowed her head, reverent to the occasion, carried by the moment, honoring the dead. Nodding with the eulogizer. Gripping a hanky as the near-and-dear filed past. Renie was glad for the open casket, stopping longer than those who paused briefly and looked away. It was, after all, a first acquaintance.

Flowers banked the altar and by the coffin bowed the children, clutching the box as they had its occupant. Today's children were no longer kept at home by sitters, as if their parents were briefly having fun. The little boy wore the pain of forced indoors at school. The little girls sniffled, one using a crumpled tissue, the other an edge of skirt.

Father, when you were at rest at last, did you lie beneath

an oval lid and did flowers grow on its embankment and did my mother cry?

Beside the children the widower gave himself to grief. Renie stared at the fine man, balding, pin-striped and rep-tied, at his dignity, bereaved but not yet bereft. You who held a woman nightly, what is your need compared to mine?

Soon he would be available, left over. Renie reflected on the remains and the remainder. A man with a young family would want a woman soon. She had an abundance of self to give away. She would go to the cemetery and to their home. And if not this family, there would be others, other victims of demise. And perhaps it would fall to her to complete the equation. The gift of solace would be hers. Let the teachers laugh. They had before.

# DIMINISHING RETURNS

———

Rhona was feeling less herself. Mornings she'd fix break-fast, trayed, displayed, and played to four Felder appetites. Afternoons were errands, errands. By dinner there was just enough of Rhona to cater a little nutrition into the family. As the last of the greasy water gurgled, she felt it taking her down, down the drain.

Maybe she ought to see a doctor, never seen by the Felders. They saw them, to be sure, at cocktails or tennis, and at conferences that brought tax deductions and doctors together and gave doctors' wives respite from doctors' lives.

Dr. Felder was not a keeper-upper himself. Rather, his disciples kept up with him: nephrologist Horace Moriah Felder, physician's physician, consultant to WHO, consultant to consultants.

Tonight, even conversation seemed an effort. The meal, so carefully prepared, seemed too quickly dispatched. The roast was congealed in its juices, the salad settled to a few wilted leaves.

"Morey," Rhona tried. "Do you like the apple relish?" He had probably lost interest in apples as far back as Eve.

The doctor leaned back, baldness against blue velvet, smiling the smile that began his career. He had not had time to learn another. He fingered his short gray beard. "Fine, fine. Hmm . . . perhaps a bit more vinegar . . ." the last line canceled the first.

A son and daughter faced each other, their elders squaring the ends. Her tongue brushing her lower lip, the girl concentrated her french fries into a log cabin, and when it was built, her brother leaned over to knock it down.

"Quit it! Make him stop!"

Like every younger child, stopping her older sibling was the longing of her life. If her brother would stop growing, even, to let her catch up!

Rhona sighed. She had planned to share the day's events, but morning seemed a long time past. She wished dinner was the end of the day, instead of a comma before bedtime.

"This weakness, Morey. Do you think iron pills? At my age, perhaps my blood . . ."

"Iron pills, rusty blood," cracked Andy, teenage author of verbless quips.

But the tape recorder came with dessert, and already Morey was dictating Rx's for the sick world.

For forty minutes Rhona had been standing outside the striped tent that umbrellaed the backyard wedding. Wiping the gathering beads, she regretted the long sleeves the morning had falsely signaled. June's noon was warm for twenty minutes, hot for forty.

Morey's "right back" was, as usual, relative. Where was a welcome face? None of the St. Bart's senior staff elbowed the crowd. Rhona's drink was watered in melted ice, merely an annoyance at midday, when it was needed less.

"Why, you must be Mrs. Felder." The intern's recognition unctuated her burn. The young man shone in a white sports jacket that pointed up his tan. Rhona could see medicine would flatter him.

"What's it like to be married to the great man? Always in the thick of things! I bet, Mrs. Felder, yours is The Life!" But a skinny young thing hallooed him away, and that was all of The Life! that touched him.

At St. Bart's, Stephanie Connors expedited Dr. Felder's appointments, the plane reservations, the researched quotes, felt-tipped in red banners. When the secretary vacationed, Rhona rolled in to take her place.

"Stephanie *and* Rhona, you lucky bastard." Stu Altman, Morey's young associate, was candid in his envy. "Hell, Morey. How did you develop a wife like that?"

"That's matrimony, Stu," Morey, glancing up, seemed to be looking down. "Married so long, we're one person!"

All she had seen of her husband that morning was his floored underwear, proof of a corporeal mate. Now she plugged in the tape recorder on Stephanie's desk and listened to his voice.

"Good morning, Rhona," the tape reeled. "Don't forget to RSVP the Strangs, cocktails okay, dinner's out . . . letters, please, to all junior staff regarding excellent reports." Rhona gathered herself for the rapid notes. "Did you pick up books reserved at library? . . . Check long-range for Nashville . . . I may need more short-sleeved shirts . . ."

The phone rang. "Excuse me, Morey." Rhona flipped off one mechanism for the other.

"Dr. Felder's office."

"Hello, hello," came the reply.

"Dr. Felder's office."

"Hello, is anyone there?" the voice repeated.

Couldn't he hear? Rhona shouted her hellos, who is calling please, and still he stuttered hello, hello.

"Dr. Felder's office," Rhona reaffirmed. "Who is calling please?" At the other end was an abrupt click.

This was the third badly connected call that morning. But when Rhona dialed Repair, it, too, "helloed, helloed." So even the telephone company had poor service. It was small consolation.

Her head and feet seemed miles apart. The vaporous sensation frightened her. She felt like a picture she had seen of Alice. Was it before or after she had passed through the Rabbit Hole?

*　*　*

When her husband was away, Rhona served the evening meal by the fire or on the patio, depending on the season, or occasionally in front of the TV. On their evenings together, the family used the dining room. Morey felt this developed social skills, and certainly sharpened table manners.

It was true that informal meals did not lean toward conversation. When Rhona asked her daughter about school, she'd "Shh, this is the good part," a comic book by her plate or a favorite comic on the screen.

But when Sparks stretched out on her stomach to draw, the words flowed with the quick, swift lines. "How is this? Does it look like the pony in the Marshalls' meadow? Tawny enough?"

Andy, enigmatic one, was tall, redheaded, silent. Blessedly, girls hadn't found him yet. The longer he stayed in sports, the safer he would be. He was such a late talker, Morey had had him tested, but his hearing and mind were fine. "Must be a listener," the otologist had laughed. "We sure could use more of 'em!"

Lately Rhona wondered about her own hearing, her own speech. She'd eavesdrop on fellow shoppers levying their resentment of spoilage under Saran. She watched a stout matron hand the produce man two rotten tomatoes, a soundless wrath hanging over the woman like a cartoon balloon without print. While Rhona dealt out coupons at the checkout, the register spit up its tally, oblivious to her intent. Every week Rhona vowed she would speak to the cashier before it was all totaled.

She had come to the table feeling weightless. Should she tell her husband how the markets cheated their customers?

"Morey," she began, glad he had come home on the early flight.

"Daddy," their hoyden intervened.

"Morey," Rhona said again.

"Yes, Sparks," the daughter won his reply.

"Did you get what I wanted in St. Louis? You promised! Is it in your suitcase? Can I look?"

"Morey . . ."

"C'mon, Sparks. Come and get it." Twined, the doctor and the girl departed. Tears salted Rhona's eyes.

"Master of the world, a daughter's slave," the teenager observed.

The youngster, turning at the doorway, stuck at her brother a long blueberried tongue.

The rain seemed more March-like than gentle. Grayness dropped its bunting as Rhona sat in the parked vehicle outside the piano teacher's house. Every Tuesday she drove the station wagon to the next county, wondering if an hour's lesson was worth a two-hour ride. Now she leaned back against the white leather seat, eyes closed, hoping to be refreshed with a deep, short nap.

The automobile seemed in the rain more insular than ever. When she and Morey were kids in college, his Ford jalopy was their only retreat. Seated in the battered coupe, the difference in their heights was allayed, Morey towering over her with his strength, his determination.

Cars were notorious refuges, but more talking took place in them, she bet, than romance. They had painted across its dented side "The MoreRhon," a spoof of his famed intelligence. In it Morey painted his dreams. Oiling his strategies with scholarships, fellowships, and grants, Morey Felder would pull himself up by his IQ alone.

Rhona snapped awake as her little girl bounced out of the house, an hour to the minute. The first half hour Sparks exercised the scales. The second was given to repertoire. While the child played, the teacher wrote orders for home practice in Sparks's notebook. They rarely talked.

Straining to see through the torrents, Rhona tempted Sparks's interest in next week's community concert. A child who studies music ought to hear it. But, the lesson behind her, Sparks chattered above her mother, above the rain, ranging from Girl Scouts to her handsome gym teacher and, with rippled joy, to the coming horse show.

* * *

The specialist was restless, his watch-watching a nervous twitch. Cocktail parties bored him. They were a lifeline for many medical people, locked in one-to-one pairings, hungry for gossip like any boxed-in housewife. But for Morey, parties were a Hippocratic duty. He felt obliged to be a resource, a fount, whenever his colleagues gathered.

Now he detached himself from his associates and their vapid wives. "Rhona," he patted the stubbed beard as he plumbed his memory. "Have you found the source for McGill's quote? Wonder if Archives has it? . . . By the way, did you renew *Physician's Digest*? . . . and, Rhona dear, you'll see about Super Savers to Bogotá . . ."

Suddenly Rhona felt her mind click, like a typewriter when its ribbon runs out. Oh, she could never carry all his messages in her head. The small cocktail bag, chained on her shoulder, held cosmetic pick-me-ups. How could she have forgotten the notepad, the pen, to assist her husband as he carved out his life?

"Last night's wine was not up to quality, I thought, didn't you? Let's give a Rothschild a try . . ."

Rhona opened the silver pouch, found the eyebrow pencil, moistened the tip with her tongue. Competently, she spread out her left hand. On the palm she wrote,

"McGill
Digest sub.
Wine
Super Savers"

and, paralyzed with stiffness, carried the hand writing home.

It was the rarest of days. This weekend was Morey's gift to his family; the answering service had been warned; Rhona had cooked and packed; the children seemed less Arab, less Israeli. Even the weather was cooperating.

Her husband restored himself at sea. His favorite topic was the primal quality of the ocean, primordially, the bounding waves. "From inception, or conception, if you will, the fetus, and later the embryo, learns to bob. Its earliest patterning, thus, is the movement within the uterine fluid."

Morey liked to leave by seven. The drive to the mooring was an hour, with luck. "Let's go, shipmates!" A "Go Go Quakers" sweatshirt topped his rope-tied jeans and sockless deck shoes. No one, he assured his wife, would recognize Moriah Felder in his dissolute attire.

"Can I handle the jib?" Sparks pushed. "You'll see, I can do it."

"Okay, first mate. No galley duty this trip."

Andy hauled fishing gear and tarpaulin, a poncho folded neatly in his back pocket.

The weekend was certain to be prophylactic. Sun, salt, a good book, her family. The sloop had seemed an extravagance, but today Rhona was grateful for its excuse, thankful they had no phone at sea. All at once she recalled a line from school, "No man is an island." Had Donne meant women as well? Swinging the picnic on one arm, her mending in the other, Rhona joined her relatives in the gunning wagon.

"Morey," Rhona brought up the latest tale at St. Bart's. "Have you heard about Livingstone's new wife?" The octogenarian had not caused a stir by marrying. After all, marriage was his pastime. The surprise lay in his young wife's obvious pleasure.

Moriah Felder leaned against the spar. A journal rested loosely in his hand, his mind sailing off the waves, long past the rolling vessel. The doctor was at a meeting, a conference, a lecture . . . one that had been or one that was coming, no child returned to mysteries maternal.

Rhona stopped. Andy, working the *Times* puzzle, monitored a fishing pole by his side. She reached for her mending, took the thread between her lips, held the needle to the light. Sun squinted her perception. She aimed the thread toward the needle's eye.

Andy's gaze was felt as a hand itself. A power rose from the boy, as transitory as an actinism, touching her chillingly with its strength. Had she imagined the intimation, almost an admonition? He had returned to the black-and-white boxes, black and white, clearcut, converging lines of sense and order.

Rhona looked for the spool in which to replace the needle. But her lap had emptied. The floating wicker basket had become a buoy atop the waves. Below it, a school of socks made its way gently to the deep.

Chip Blackwood whistled the *Times* into their mailbox, leapt to touch the willow bough, almost low enough to meet his reach, patted the Felder springer, and sprinted down the path to his bike.

Rhona smiled her welcome at the door. Tom Sawyer on a ten-speed.

Chip always had a word for her, a pat for Queenie, a wave for the willow bough. Today the paper slipped into the slot, and Chip played out his routine—pat, wave, hop on the bike, away. Not a word for the lady of the house.

He wasn't a rude child. Why, Chip Blackwood had been coming to the Felders ever since his older brothers were the news purveyors.

"Hi there, Chip! How's the family?" Her call had surely reached him, but the paperboy, gazing either through or past her, continued on his way.

Rhona suddenly went cold. Come, come, old girl, she scolded herself. Well, she knew teenage boys. He was merely preoccupied.

All day the numbness came and went. It started with needles in her fingers, echoed in her toes. Can all twenty digits fall asleep at once? She shook the appendages till the needling took itself off, leaving the strange numbness in the endings.

En route to Bogotá to deliver a paper, Morey could not be reached.

Rhona moved through the day, seeing to the dust, seeing

to the weeds, setting out clean jars for tomorrow's preserves, matching socks two by two by two. Andy was off with the school band, Sparks at a pajama party.

On the kitchen table the tape recorder replaced the girl's customary note. "Mom, be sure to get me a notebook, two colored pencils, one blue and one red. We're having a test, and Miss McDermott said Don't Forget!"

Rhona winced. A child of the century. She would miss the ingenuous, misspelled scrawls.

Light-headed with airiness, Rhona bent to the teak liquor cabinet. Profiled in Ludwigs, it opened to a tinkle of Moonlight Sonata. Rhona selected a Kentucky bourbon. She remembered the bluegrass country of the Kentucky Derby. Blue grass. Blue. A haze of color for horses and riders. Was it five, no seven, years ago?

"You must be Dr. Felder's wife," the Rhetts and Scarlets purred. Then at the jockey's urge, the horses had kicked off to the blue hue of the day.

Rhona took the bottle to the bedroom, returned to the kitchen for ice. Ice, she giggled. I don't want a few cubes, I want ice! The refrigerator trays filled the bucket with their chatter. Now to meet the bottle by the bed.

Nice ice. In the glass, bluegrass.

See, m'boy? I know the lingo!

It was late, the clock too fuzzy to tell the time. Rhona stared vacuously at the tidy slippers footed by the bed, the robe on the chaise. At the open window, the breeze pushed the curtains, but it neither braced her face nor rustled her hair. She stretched her arms to meet it, withdrew to hug herself. Rhona's numbness now was total.

Sinking beneath the blanket's waffle, Rhona reflected on her son, sixteen, self-contained. Sparks? The girl had traded tape for her umbilical.

And Morey . . .

Nullified, she closed her eyes.

Ah, Dr. Felder, yes, we are indeed one person. We are you.

* * *

In the morning when Rhona rose, the bed was smooth, the sheet taut, the pillow puffed. She floated to the master bath, turned the nozzle, and let the steam rise slowly, slowly through her.

She squiggled the toothpaste to the brush. Drifted toward the mirror. Looked up to view the routine polish. Recoiled.

Ha, ha, here's a good one for you, my son, my son.

Hysteria tinged her mirth.

Faceless image. . . . Soundless scream!

# TO SAVE AND PROTECT

All the days and nights of plotting, the haranguing, bargaining, cajoling. How Anya's Grandfather worked to get Tante Leah off his hands. If only her aunt were not so stubborn, Grandfather might soften his iron will. "Why was this woman so independent?" he shouted, rattling the teacups. "Who is she, past bloom, past choosing?" he pounded the table with his fist, making Anya jump. Tante Leah had refused every matchmaker, scorned every match.

Each night with dinner came Grandfather's boastful conquests—money, money! But with the fruit and tea came the plans for Tante Leah. Grandfather disposed of property, cash, and women's lives.

There had been the hunchback whom even prosperity had not straightened out. The Litvak with the glass eye. From him emitted fetid cabbage and boiled fish. Up from the country was Karl the widower whose sensuous beard parted on juicy lips. More than his eleven children, Karl himself needed a strong mother.

Tonight was Mische. "That bore with the wart on his nose?" Tante Leah sneered. "Mische the *pische*."

"Mische the *mensch*," Grandfather corrected. "Money covers up warts."

"Should I keep my eyes closed then, except when counting money?" Tante Leah spat on them all, could make a snake look meek.

Before each social evening, Tante Leah instructed Anya to hide behind the parlor door. "You'll bring in tea when the stroking starts." And Anya was to break in rudely when the talk headed toward anything that might be serious.

As Anya peeked from behind the portieres, waiting for her cue, she mimicked that night's suitor, his limp, his twitch, or his shortened breath.

Ah, but Anya knew the gentleness her aunt could not display. Those lips forever pinched, and her brows pinched too, above an arched nose. Perhaps Tante Leah had been squeezed by some wicked giant. She even moved with little jerks. Not her walk or talk, nor how she sat or ate, was ever an easy flow. She would come to Anya at night, to the orphan in her charge, to scold her badness and hear her day. Then she'd hold her on her lap and hug and rock her, although Anya was already twelve, no longer a little child.

To her needlework went Tante Leah's other passion. If not for suitors her caress, then for fine linen, silk thread. From that devotion sprang embroidered pillow slips, cloths that dressed tables, monogrammed undergarments of imported batiste, her own of a delicacy to make one blush. A dowry Anya would put to her cheek, pat gently, wondering when she, too, would be a woman.

Before Shabbos was the rhythm of their bath. Here rose Tante Leah's essence. With gentle fingers her aunt massaged her in the vast tub. Soon, from a surprising depth, a low crooning would begin, nearly a sob, summoned from the sweetness of her soul. The lullaby, "*Orchis chornya, orchis goudnya . . . oh those huge dark eyes . . . ,*" was a purity Tante Leah hid from the world. She swayed as the music rose with the steam, gathering Anya in her strong hands, buffing her as if a gem. As she twisted Anya's long black hair to examine the nape, the ears, the woman's hands kept tempo with the Russian melody. Serene as warm water the voice fell, music and love entwined. Then, patting Anya with enormous towels, Tante Leah giggled at their extravagance, a conspiracy against tight-fisted Grandfather. Finally Tante Leah sprayed her all over with great pink puffs of scent.

As they dressed for the Friday dinner, Anya studied her aunt's frail figure, the narrow ribs, the flat inverted nipples. The woman's elbows and knees, red and scaly, her ankles chicken-fine, no legs for twining. The chest was caven, protected by round shoulders. From her cloven niche a blue-black forest sprang to her navel. Unlike the thin strands pinned to Leah's scalp, it spread with electric curls. Anya compared the nubile growth to her own silk down seeping into womanhood, and her aunt's hairy discs to the itching titties nuzzling her sheets at night, begging to be soothed. When she rubbed them, her vagina echoed the tickle, but Anya knew she was to save and protect the female parts of her body for the mysteries of adult life.

Shabbos dinner is over. The dishes cleared. The candles melted to the quick. Grandfather snores in his study, an old man's discourse with his dreams. On Shabbos lights rest, stoves rest, and stomachs, too, are told to expect little, for food is cold from onset to sunset of this holy day. Grandfather sees the day for sleep, telling his family he is behind doors to study the good books. Quiet, quiet. Set off no storms in Grandfather's haven. Anya roams the high-ceilinged flat on Kozla Street, rustles not a skirt or sash, tries not to snag the tiny precious objects which Tante Leah has strewn on all the shelves and tables. At the red velvet draperies, Anya peeks out at Poles hurrying against the winter. She rocks by the fire, speaks in whispers.

When Tante Leah goes for a nap, Anya lifts each picture, mirror, book, Chinese figure, porcelain bowl, and brass tray, gently, gently turning round these pieces from Uncle Joseph's travels. Uncle Joseph, the German uncle, the family aristocrat! Uncle Joseph who authors books in gold-lit Hebrew, boxed and revered on Grandfather's cherry desk. Uncle Joseph, not blessed with *kinder*, children, with only his dear frau to miss him when his journal takes him to distant lands.

As Anya cradles each treasure of her uncle's journeys, she imagines the city of its origin. Where had this good man been, this most learned of all her uncles, when he'd bargained for this trinket or that?

Anya reaches to the high shelves for luminous volumes. Secretly she sniffs the heavy leather, heart beating against being caught, the bindings older than Grandfather himself. Tea-colored pages crackle as they turn.

When Tante Leah awakens, she is full of grumbles. "Anyashka," she moans, "the Poles dance and sing on their Sabbath, pray on Sunday mornings, and have high times later. And here we are, locked in, expected to think holy thoughts. If only we could at least read the prayer book."

"The Hebrew, you know how hard it is. We are lucky to be spared the square letters. Cousins Avram and Roishe still need tutors, and I heard Tante Malke worry their bar mitzvahs will be when they are truly grown."

Her aunt smiles. Anya both hates and adores her wicked cousins.

"To hear them chant, it hurts my ears," Anya says. "If prayers are for men, why do they have such tarnished voices? You and I, Tante, we would be birds singing to heaven if only it were permitted."

The clocks tick in soft accord, working despite the Sabbath, helpless to push the long hours more swiftly toward day's end.

For weeks they had been polishing the *Pesach* silver, taking from upper shelves the *Pesach* dishes. Soon Grandfather would halt his battles with her spinster aunt, and then Kozla Street would be full of life, filled with all the Kaplans, the cousins, the aunts, and the uncles, all the uncles. Like Russian dolls, *matreshkas,* that opened one upon the other, the uncles sat in rows of assorted sizes, Joseph, Judah, Zaydel, Boris, Hersch. At the great feasts, the eves of holy days, the eating into the long nights of Passover, they sat at their end of the table, men allied with father or father-in-law, bowed in prayer, their voices raised in ritual song and sorrow, those bent toward mischief prodding each other with trickery, those molded in somberness scowling like Grandfather.

Anya was kept on her toes when the relatives were there, hopping to serve them. How she admired mustaches twisted by dandies, the city uncles, or whiskers wild and free on chins of the pious. How pale and white they were, those indoor faces, except when schnapps tinged a nose or cheek. Only peasants were drunkards, Tante Leah had said, but oh how the uncles swigged the wine sanctioned by the holiday. Anya kept watch on these men who broke her days with women.

As Anya was an orphan, she was treated kindly by her aunts and uncles, but her cousins used it against her. Cousin Avram was the devil himself, hissing "stupid orphan" whenever he passed. Avram's shaggy hair pointed in two tufts above a cunning brow, eyes which seemed always to watch the action, to anticipate it, to be a jump ahead. He could slip a banana peel beneath a blind man's faltering step, so great was his scorn of God. And crabs and toads in Anya's bed were the expected when Avram was around. There was something of the hyena on his face, a wildness deaf to the curbs of natural folk.

But Avram was a saint next to his brother, Cousin Roishe, with hands out for any girl, catching a buttock here or there and winning for it Uncle Boris's leering praise. He was as lumbering as Avram was nimble. His were the wits of an ass. Not a year older than she, Roishe relished Tanya's terror, taunting her, keeping her from tattling even to Tante Leah. But her aunt was on to the barbarians, glowering with disgust, snapping a sharp towel across their backsides when she caught them at their pranks.

Cigar smoke filled the diningroom, despite the pious uncles' pleas, "Not on *Yom Tov*!" Grandfather said not even God could keep from him a good cigar. As the elders reached for the prayer books, peering over the ancient dialogues, Tante Leah leaned down and whispered to her charge, "Ah, Anyashka, the Hebrew, how hard it is. Avram and Roishe, the dolts, will never learn no matter the *gelt* spent to teach them!"

Anya felt what must be a dead fish beneath her skirts,

leaped, but was pinned by Avram's elbow. Crawling up and up was the hand of Roishe, rubbing against her knitted hose, reaching for her thigh. Tears sprang to her eyes as she struggled to kick the demon beneath the table. All about the festive board the elders were rocking in divine meditation, shawls wrapping heads and shoulders. Just then Tante Leah clutched her hand to snap her away into the small red parlor for the woman's worship.

And the world of men was shut.

When, at last, at fifteen, Cousin Avram could become a man, Grandfather paused in his quest for Tante Leah's groom. Customary at thirteen, the bar mitzvah had been deferred, the rabbi looking the other way.

"Ha! He was bribed!" Tante Leah sneered.

The occasion was enough to stir Grandfather with great effort to share her cousin's special day. So today Avram would be a man. Would the evil of his tainted soul fall away under the new blessings?

Grandfather was to be taken to *shul,* the synagogue, by his eldest sons, Judah from Krakow and Joseph from Leipzig, to serve in Avram's quorum. Again the women swept and baked, nervous to welcome the worshipers, to feed their natural hungers. In the kitchen more than onions made Anya cry. How she longed to disguise herself, wear a joke-store beard, bear witness to Avram's mystical change. How could a boy become a man in one morning? What magic would the rabbi perform? And why were the women kept from the synagogue and forced to stay at home? Where was a just God?

Behind the kitchen door Anya peeked at the returning entourage, hats kept on by tradition, pouring schnapps as though the *shul* had been a desert. The bar mitzvah boy himself had returned subdued from his ordeal. Perhaps Avram's elflocks had been trimmed for the occasion. Perhaps sanctity had entered his heart at last. Avram's side curls had been twisted in rags by Tante Malke, Roishe had tattled, and was given Avram's fist to his cheek for his big mouth. Anya could see a mustache shading Avram's upper lip. If Avram was now a man, would he by nightfall grow a full beard?

The food and wine, the toasts of merriment, more drunkenness than Anya had seen on a Polish holiday!

"To Leah's groom, whoever he may be!" Uncle Boris started the needling.

"Hush, Boris," Tante Malke was sensitive to her sister's plight. Had not she, too, succumbed to the matchmaker, and then to Boris?

Tante Leah looked to her father, fearing a new onslaught of nuptial nagging, but Grandfather was snoring like a peasant, drunk in no time. Uncle Joseph, with a wink to Anya, lifted the old man and leaned him on his shoulder, leading him to bed. Uncle Joseph, as kind as he was wise, and always, always with a special word for Anya. Tante Leah said it was because he had adored his sister, Anya's mother, long taken by the influenza, but Anya didn't believe that. She knew better. He adored *her*.

That night Kozla Street was a railroad full of snores. The aunts and uncles made their way to rooms they had used as children, doubling up the cousins wherever mats or beds could be found. Cousin Avram and Cousin Roishe took Tante Leah's room on the other side of Anya's and Tante Leah's shared bathroom, with Tante Leah saying tonight Avram deserved the larger room, and she didn't mind sleeping in the little alcove.

As water rushed into the tub next door, Anya listened to Cousin Avram singing, singing! Why his voice was that of an angel. Surely God had altered him after all!

Smiling, letting sleep take her, she was serenaded by the saint in the tub on the other side of the wall. Suddenly there was bathroom light pouring into her room, and as Anya rose to shut the door, a figure, in white, white, was striding toward her bed. A ghost! Anya tried to scream but now another hand gagged her mouth. In the dark the white figure slowly unwound the huge towel, a naked devil. Avram!

As Roishe pinned her down to the bed, Avram laughed

like one possessed, waving a stick of flesh in her face. "For you, for you, wretched orphan!" Scream, scream, the wretched orphan. "The tool of *men*," he roared. And here now was Tante Leah holding her, calming her, as Avram, howling with laughter, swung the upright flesh toward his room.

In the morning when all the relatives were preparing to depart, Tante Leah made excuses for Anya, keeping her in bed, saying she was unwell. Uncle Joseph sent up his card, scrawled with "Come and visit!" Imagine Leipzig and the German relatives! Tante Leah had put hot coals wrapped in cloths on Anya's gnawing stomach. Her head throbbed, and throughout her groin were hammers. She had been cursed, cursed by the devil hiding in Avram. Poor Tante Malke, fated to be the mother of such a maleficent. How had such an impure creature found his way to the good Kaplans? Why had he reviled her, Anya, with his poison?

Anya writhed in her bed. Now Tante Leah pressed compresses to her head, spoke of sending for a bloodsucker if the girl felt no peace by morning. Doctors had put such vermin onto her beloved mother, but even they could not pull the fate from her failing soul.

"No, No, Tante. No bloodsucking. You'll see it is only too much feasting. A little rest, tomorrow will be fine."

It was night, the house as still as a grave. Anya rose abruptly from sleep, a wet stickiness beneath her. No, she had not soiled herself, whoever heard of a thirteen year old wetting the bed? She explored the dampness, put it to her nose. Blood? Blood! She pulled the chain of her bulb, rushed to the mirror. A stain as large as a wound covered the front of her nightgown, trickling to her thighs. She raised the offending cloth, the bubbles of her breasts quivering in the chill. She ran her hand between her thighs, inside the forbidden darkness. Never touch, Tante Leah had warned! But she had, she had! Pretending even to herself to be asleep, how often she had patted the velvet there, violated that private delicacy.

Wicked fingers had played tattoos in the dark, stroking a throbbing sweetness.

And now the blood!

"I'm dying, dying!" she sobbed, dripping blood into the little alcove where Tante Leah slept. "Help me, Tante," she shook her aunt awake.

"Save me," Anya was hysterical. "I'm dying, bleeding to death!"

Her aunt snapped awake. She stared at the growing stain.

And she slapped Anya hard across the cheek.

The sting hurt more than anything Anya had ever known. So her aunt understood her sin. She had defied Tante Leah's warning. Not enough to die of hemorrhage. Anya would die of shame.

Then Tante Leah was hugging her, laughing, rocking her big girl on her lap.

"Darling, Anyashka, don't worry, don't worry. I am sorry to slap you. As my mother did to me, all girls fend off the Evil Eye this way!"

Anya sobbed into her aunt's frail breast. An orphan who did not understand, life ever more a mystery, here among relatives who were no real family.

"Darling, Anya, Anya," Tante Leah smoothed her hair, rocked her, kissed her cheeks, kissed away the tears.

"Darling, don't you understand? It's wonderful. You are a woman. Today you are a woman.

"Now you are one of us."

# CRAVING LUSTER

Butterflies quiver across my middle as Miss Fielding sets aside Geometry and says, "Now, class, 'Lady of the Lake.'"

The students moan as they lift their desks to scramble inside for the poem, and dart mean looks toward me. I am the only one who can find the metaphors, and Miss Fielding conducts this class as if for me. This secret code is known only to Sir Walter Scott, Miss Louise Fielding, and her star pupil.

I brighten with excitement, but in walks smug Carol Herlihy doing the work of the office this period. She hands Miss Fielding a note, and the teacher reads the name on it with concern. She summons me to her desk, whispering, "Nothing bad, I hope." What is so urgent, what disaster, to interrupt school?

The message is from Poppa. "Meet me at Park Street in an hour. We are going to see the president."

All the way to Park Street Station the trolley chants The President, The President. Whenever that warm voice poured from our radio, no phone rang, mothers stopped dusting. Kids delayed homework, knew not to play. Hushed, we huddled about the box, solemn as in synagogue, to hear FDR soothe his flock.

"Even from a wheelchair he keeps us safe," Poppa would say.

The President! What is more unfathomable, Poppa taking time from work or taking me out of school? Do not imagine, his stern face says when I step from the trolley, this a day

merely to skip school. Poppa knows when education is better
served.

"Why today, Poppa, why here?" I try breathlessly to match
his stride. This Poppa who walks miles to work, miles on the
beach, who maybe invented the art of walking, what matter
his twelve-year-old daughter runs two quick steps to each
long stride?

"It's his election campaign, his last, they say. Too sick for
another term. But he kept his promise, kept the bombs away.
Soon the war will end, even if it's the end of Mr. Roosevelt."

Across The Common, past the Frog Pond, over the green
scrolled iron bridge spanning swan boat fairyland, past bums
on benches or under elms. To let me catch my breath, Poppa
stops for hot chestnuts from an Italian vendor.

"The President is coming!" Poppa shouts, as if being
Italian was being deaf. Shivering, he tugs up the old tweed
collar against the chill, his cheeks pink against the wind.

Poppa holds my arm and drags me onward, toward base-
ball's Fenway Park, erupting with a thrusting mob.

"Sit a minute on the curb," he relents. "I forgot you are
not used to it. In the Old Country five, ten miles was
nothing. How spoiled Americans are!"

Throngs pour from the subway to ford Kenmore Square.
Mounted patrols keep order under watchful eyes. Only
three o'clock and the ceremonies not till evening, but
people rush early for a good bird's-eye view. Flags are sold
and waved; a firecracker pops somewhere; Fourth of July
in November.

Caught in the crowd pushing me headlong, I shout,
"Poppa, hold my hand, I'm losing you!" and I am four again,
being lifted to the Flying Horses or out of giant waves, in
Poppa's strong hands, Poppa's little girl.

"Keep an orderly line, order here now, order," the bull-
horns blare. Snatches of patriotic music. Kate Smith. Morton
Downey. Vendors hawking patriotic buttons, programs, sou-
venirs, hot dogs.

Inside the park carpenters are tacking finishing touches to

the backboard and bunting to the platform in center field. By it is a ramp for the presidential car. Enormous posters of The President and The Governor hide the old scores. Floodlights are laid down, the bases loaded with them, and above the field wave strings of small bulbs.

"Coca-Cola, popcorn, peanuts!" We scramble up, up to the bleachers, like an ordinary day at the ball park.

A very fat man on the bench behind us waves a huge cigar and, in the spirit rising all around, leans down to offer Poppa a puff. No, no, Poppa demurs. "How about for the little lady?" the smoker guffaws. Alongside of us four nuns, habits spread across knees, fondle beads across their chests, while on the bench below an old couple argue nervously, one voice attacking, the other defending.

Poppa shrugs and looks at me with irritation. Was this a time to quarrel?

Picnics come out and flasks are passed. "Hot dogs! Popcorn here!" In peaked caps and short white jackets, boys skip the steep steps, balancing boxes on straps swinging around their necks. The bleachers steadily fill. In reserved front rows Gold Star mothers and wives take wooden chairs, and ushers hasten more folding chairs onto the field. "No more, no more," the loud-speakers holler, but security gives way to the public need.

Some women toss fliers of Earl Browder, while others pass out "Protect our Churches" and "Fight Communism" and "Keep America Free!" I gather the leaflets in my arms to read at home in the bathroom. By six o'clock even the aisles are filled, everyone willing to squeeze one more in beside them. The spirit of hoopla! Just another day at the ball game, folks. An afternoon for sun and fun.

But it would be night soon, and stillness.

Again there would descend the hush that glowed around radios in millions of reverent homes.

Sensing a need to fill the wait, a parade of politicians takes turns with the fan of mikes. "Blah, blah, blah." Called up next is a Gold Star mother who, the emcee booms, "has lost

not one, folks, not two, not three, but FOUR stalwart sons."
Stamping! Clapping! A roaring cheer!

By eight forty-five the audience is gently stamping. Beat,
beat. At last the dugout doors fly open, and a row of cars
spills out. A slow cavalcade of open black autos rolls across
center field. The crowd goes mad with delirium. The fat man
pounds Poppa, "He's here, he's here!" Shouts rent the sky.
Hats are tossed. Women fling hankies. No ball players these,
but The President himself, circling the park in the lead black
limo, like the head of a funeral cortege. Around and around,
waving the bent fedora, peering over rimless glasses, huddled
beneath the familiar black cape, as in the *Pathé News*. Grinning and waving his hat, playing the picture of health, as if
we didn't see the darkness below his specs.

A flourish, a strike of the band and "God Bless America."
The nuns bow and cross themselves. The fat man stomps on
his cigar. The couple halt in midfight. Hands are placed on
hearts. All rise to love of land and leader.

The front auto rolls up to the ramp, and seated in it still,
The President takes the mike to address Boston and the
nation.

"My friends," he begins. "I'll be brief. Radio time costs
money." Laughter. "The only thing to fear is fear itself."
Shrieks, stamps. Sly references to his opponent, never dropping the name of Dewey. Applause. Waving the cigarette
holder. Pausing for effect. Widely grinning. But I am no
longer looking at my President, watching instead my father.

"The President, The President of the United States," he
says over and over, fat tears running down his red cheeks.

With the historic visit over, Poppa circumvents crowded
Kenmore Station by retracing our steps toward town. Back
through the starlit park, taking time now to peer at beamed
ceilings behind purple bow windows. A sharp chill cuts
through as though the weather had held for FDR. As I shiver,
Poppa unwinds his plaid scarf, wraps it around me, puts one
of my icy hands in his, tucks them both inside his pocket. It's

okay. No one to see me walking with Poppa holding my hand. I squeeze his in the pocket, and he squeezes back.

Past the golden-domed State House, admiring the fancy Baptist Temple, to stop at last at Dini's Sea Grille, to celebrate, to stuff ourselves with broiled fish.

"Squeeze a little lemon on it. Gives it flavor," he says.

"Poppa, what was it like in the Old Country where no one is ever spoiled? How was it for you then? And wouldn't you like to be? I mean, spoiled? Just once?"

## II

My daughter sits with eyes wide asking how it was to be a child. If one could only remember, one could be a child forever.

Spoiled! Spoiled was what fish got when left too long. Spoiled was the milk in my mother's buckets if the sun shone too hot too soon. On her broad back a yoke held the swinging pails, small bells ringing as she swayed.

Spoiled? It was not a word for children. Responsibility came early. Nor were there "teens," spoiled by permission of the glands. You were a man before you were a man. How could we be spoiled when legs were for walking and a back for bending and one's head for keeping one's wits?

I had so many brothers who came and went that I, the youngest, sometimes lost track of them. All gone away before I could walk, it seemed, and returned mainly as legends. "This is how Jacob did this," or "your brother Shmuel did it that way," my mother compared me to men now married and already fathers. I was a boy trying to be all my brothers, such a family tree to climb!

In our Belorussian village, a manor stood on a hill like a lighthouse beaming toward wealth. If even one man lived so, could not someday one of us? I peeked in lighted windows at their richness, as we looked in tonight on Beacon Street. I was spoiled by rich dreams. But my family was so poor it was for us the temple charity box was marked, us and the trees for Palestine. As others prepared for Sabbath, my mother dragged her empty buckets home. Others lit candles that flickered like the windows in the manor, but we had no candles, no twisted bread, no wine. Not even that spoiled.

Those lonely days there was little daylight in dark Russia, little tallow to be used frivolously. I turned to hands instead of eyes. First, whittling a stick. Then sculpting soft wood. In the dark I let my fingers shape, then tell me how it was shaped, as the blind do Braille.

My father stayed in bed, coughing, snarling, sleeping. He came out to sit in a dot of sun when there was one. Once I shouted, "Get out of bed! Why does my mother go to work?" He rose in bed, his red hair a porcupine of quills, his beard as well. He found the strength to lift a wooden chair. He hurled it at me, but it hit the hearth and sprang into flames. Then he and the wood hissed and simmered down. The next day I began working by my mother's side and left him to his failing light.

We kept to ourselves out of shame. Not even the rabbi called. But one day I heard he was depriving his own livelihood by directing good Jews away. Men going into the army were suddenly going in another direction. You took a little ride, hidden in a lorry, and hoped it would take you to an ocean. They used feet, they rode under stacks of hay, they evaporated like milk from a pail left open.

# III

Poppa worked seven days a week in the Jewelers Building, leaving at dawn and returning after I was asleep. I begged Momma to let me stay up to read another chapter, hoping he would be that chapter. Did the trolley run that late, or did he, grand walker, walk that far to bed?

Momma scolded me for whining, for missing him, reminding me how lucky we were he had the work, a hungry family grateful for his care. On Saturdays we sometimes visited his airless cubby behind the protective grillwork. You had to push a secret button for him to buzz you in.

Bent to his curlicues and flowers, sculpted from a blank sheet of gold, he let the gold dust sift lightly to his high bench. When each piece was as worked as his craft would allow, he gently lifted the plaque, ring, or emblem from its padded vise. He blew lightly on the fingerprints, his own, which clouded the luster, and rubbed them away with a soft chamois. Then he lay the treasure with the others of his long day, placing it in velvet to protect the art until its presentation.

The crannies of his shop were lit by golddust, filtering to the bench, the floor, inside Poppa's rolled-up sleeves, and even caught in nostril hair. He shared his bench with another man, so silent he never looked up at visitors. He and Poppa reached to the racks nestling short beveled tools with flat round mushroom heads that fit in a cupped palm. Grasped in tight fists, the sharp metal cut the soft metal. Dust motes played beneath the dingy window as the engravers savored whatever sunlight guided the fine pick, pick of their chisels. The deaf companion, whom he called his *shtuma*, was wonderful with his hands and shouldn't be called a "dummy," a cruel taunt. Whoever worked the jewelry must be as trustworthy as he was talented. No one ever forgot the value of the goods.

At the end of each long working day Poppa used a soft handbrush to sweep the bench dust into a bucket. When it was full, the contents would be melted into molten bars. How long, Poppa, how long does it take to hoard a bucketful, how many pick, picks? Do you hear milk sloshing as the bucket fills with gold?

# IV

It is after eleven, but Poppa feels no rush toward home. From Dini's we wind through high, narrow, lantern-lit brick streets of Beacon Hill. Like the streets themselves, each house stands tall and elegant. Their lower floors, Poppa explains, are for servants, the kitchens above them, the parlor above that, and maybe no bedrooms till the fifth or sixth floor. Some doorways, overhung with protection from Boston's wicked weather, wink with bull's-eye glass. Above them shiny black shutters set off tiny iron balconies. Behind, Poppa says, are miniature gardens tended with pride. Brass knockers shine from sturdy paneled doors, each house a whisper of gentility. Here Brahmins look over their city as when they were shippers and seafarers checking their ships at sea.

We wander through Mt. Vernon Street and Louisburg Square, its little statue centered like a sentry. Meandering on Joy Street. Joy Street! To live on a street named Joy! Staring up into rooms with high ceilings, tea-paper walls, fireplaces, family portraits in oils. The night is cold and the stars little cubes in a clear dark heaven.

But Poppa is not wandering. He strides directly up to a heavy black door.

"Poppa, do you *know* these people?" I breathe in awe.

"Touch, darling, feel," Poppa lifts my icicles from his pocket.

Hand over hand we gently slide our fingers over the curly script, *Reverend Edwin A. Cochran III,* on the shiny door plate.

"Do you *know* him?" I whisper again. Will a head fling itself from the upstairs window and holler for the cops?

"As good as when I made it," he beams. "Ten years already." Poppa takes out a huge crumpled hanky from his back pocket. He leans over, blows on the nameplate, polishes it anew.

"A gruff fellow, rude when he came in, but like a lamb when he saw how it turned out. He was an Episcopal priest—they marry, you know—and I didn't know should I call him father or mister?"

Then up and down the hill, seeking the nameplates of Poppa's past. A couple of Honorables—judges, he explains—more Reverends, many M.D.s. Some had selected from Poppa's chart no-nonsense straightforward Block print, while others wished to be noted in slanting precision Script, curled in gentle Olde English, or presented to the world ornately in etched Gothic. For these fancy ones Poppa had embellished extra trills and phrases, couching the name in flowers.

In the dark Poppa gently rubs my fingers across his letters I should know who he has rubbed elbows with. Without those plates, the owners might have no claim on life, go unmarked, like soldiers in nameless graves.

The metal is cold. The houses dark. No head peers out or calls down. As house lights snap out with the late hour, only lanterns light our way. Diamonds twinkle in the sky.

With my hand inside Poppa's nubby pocket, I imagine my father walking the cold streets at night, returning to his metal offspring, buffing them for all the world.

We are alone now, the only passengers on that late trolley. I snuggle against Poppa, fighting sleep, knowing there is more and this night might never be again.

"How did you meet Momma? Was it love at first sight?"

# V

Like a miniature doll in a blue velvet bonnet, fitted coat with blue velvet collar and tiny black slippers. As shy as a rabbit. We met in an Americanization class, gathering in patriotism. I tried to strike up a little something. How lonely a man gets. Loneliness in Russia is a party next to lonely in a foreign land. Here you walk streets and never know where people are rushing, always rushing. Alone in my village I knew how to picture people's kitchens, bedrooms, even their dreams at night.

I kept wondering how to meet that lovely lady. Then one day during "The Star-Spangled Banner," she opened up! Out of that tiny mouse came the voice of a bird. The class was stunned.

If music was how to get to her, I tried, "Do you like *Madame Butterfly?*" She nodded shyly. I invited her for a cup of tea the next class. "Would you join me next week?" I barely whispered. To my surprise she accepted. I can thank *Madame Butterfly.*

I bought a Caruso recording of that sad opera, out of my food money, and next lesson before class I begged the tea shop owner to play it on the gramophone. I told her I was bringing a special lady in and how important this was to me. No expression, a plain woman, this shopkeeper. "Please, lady, you believe in Cupid, don't you?" But she didn't smile.

Of course your mother spoke little, ate nothing. Three cups of tea and still no music. I wanted to kill the stupid manager. What a fool I felt trying to court this shy frightened woman. But just as we were leaving, there was Caruso at last.

"Caruso!" I exclaimed in mock surprise. "My favorite tenor!"

I knew from her blush I'd hit gold. Caruso was hers, was everyone's then. Could I go wrong? As metal melts in the hands, your mother could now be molded.

The next week, after class, I gave her the record. "For you," I implored. "Let this be ours, between us. I knew you liked it so much, I bought it for you." So what is a little white lie? The lies of lovers even God forgives.

# VI

Such a life to learn in one evening! Momma's tales were spun in my dreams, woven into my braids, sponged onto my back, crooned to comfort fevers. Poppa's past and present waken a yearning for more, more!

Walking with him from the trolley to the apartment house, I am shaken with sadness. At the last corner before we turn toward home, I fling, "Liar! Liar! You don't work to feed us, so many mouths to feed. You don't work because you have to. You work because you love it, because you want to!" I am sobbing. "You love it more than us!"

"Fool!" he shouts back. "I have just shown you what love is. Look at all I shared with you tonight. More than I ever told another person. More than even to your mother. And it's a woman's burden to bear her husband's pain.

"Love you?" Poppa pauses, as if considering it for the first time. "Yes. Yes, I do. But children leave. Parents die. Friends move on. All that remains are hands. When I take up the work, I change it into beauty." His voice trails off and a faraway expression comes over his weary face. His beard has already grown in, and the shadows beneath his eyes are a Roosevelt's.

"Only the work remains, the memory of ourselves, and the work of our hands," he sighs.

I am crying harder now, and he brings out the buffing handkerchief and orders, "Blow!" We are at home now and Momma waves from the upstairs window. He hugs me to him as we push open the big glass double doors.

# VII

I dream that night of Poppa and his *shtuma,* the silent one, sharing his bench, humming over blank metal. Like God creating the world, they look upon what needs to be done, filling their spaces, as I, who know the metaphors, will someday fill a blank page.

AEL-4530

PS
3563
I422838
E44
1990